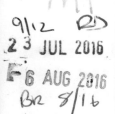

Leeds Library and Information Service

24 hour renewals

http://www.leeds.gov.uk/librarycatalogue

or phone 0845 1207271

Overdue charges may apply

Dear Reader

Once bitten, twice shy... So the old saying goes. It's one that intrigues me... How, I wondered, would a young girl respond if the man she yearned for turned her away? Wouldn't she do her utmost to steer clear of him in the future?

That's exactly how it was for Sarah, after James Benson rejected her as a vulnerable teenager. Meeting him again, years later, she's alarmed to discover that she still has feelings for him—but she can't possibly act on them.

Besides, she has way too much going on in her life, with her young half-brother and half-sister to look after, as well as the responsibility of working as a doctor in a busy emergency department.

Add to the mix the tranquil setting of a picturesque Cornish fishing village—a favourite with me—and I think you'll agree we have the perfect prescription for romance!

Love

Joanna

TAMED BY HER BROODING BOSS

BY
JOANNA NEIL

MILLS & BOON

First published in Great Britain 2012
by Mills & Boon, an imprint of Harlequin (UK) Limited.
Harlequin (UK) Limited, Eton House,
18-24 Paradise Road, Richmond, Surrey TW9 1SR

© Joanna Neil 2012

ISBN: 978 0 263 89197 3

Harlequin (UK) policy is to use papers that are natural, renewable
and recyclable products and made from wood grown in sustainable
forests. The logging and manufacturing process conform to the
legal environmental regulations of the country of origin.

Printed and bound in Spain
by Blackprint CPI, Barcelona

When **Joanna Neil** discovered Mills & Boon®, her lifelong addiction to reading crystallised into an exciting new career writing Mills & Boon® Medical™ Romance. Her characters are probably the outcome of her varied lifestyle, which includes working as a clerk, typist, nurse and infant teacher. She enjoys dressmaking and cooking at her Leicestershire home. Her family includes a husband, son and daughter, an exuberant yellow Labrador and two slightly crazed cockatiels. She currently works with a team of tutors at her local education centre to provide creative writing workshops for people interested in exploring their own writing ambitions.

Recent titles by Joanna Neil:

DR RIGHT ALL ALONG
DR LANGLEY: PROTECTOR OR PLAYBOY?
A COTSWOLD CHRISTMAS BRIDE
THE TAMING OF DR ALEX DRAYCOTT
BECOMING DR BELLINI'S BRIDE
PLAYBOY UNDER THE MISTLETOE

**These books are also available in eBook format
from www.millsandboon.co.uk**

CHAPTER ONE

'So, ARE you both okay…? Do you have everything you need?' Sarah's glance trailed over her young half-brother and half-sister, while she tried to work out if there was anything she had forgotten. It was a cool spring morning, with the wind blowing in off the sea, but the children were well wrapped up in warm jackets and trousers.

'Do you still have your money for the lunch break, Sam?' she asked, pausing to tuck a flyaway strand of chestnut-coloured hair behind her ear. He was such a whirlwind, she wouldn't have been surprised to learn that he'd lost it somewhere between the front door of the house and the school gates.

Ten-year-old Sam was clearly feeling awkward in his brand-new school uniform, but he stopped wriggling long enough to dig his hand deep into his trouser pocket.

'Yeah, it's still there.'

'Good. I'll organise some sort of account for you both with the school as soon as I can, but for now make sure you get a decent meal with what you have.' She gave Sam a wry smile. 'I don't want you to go spending it on crisps and junk food.'

His shoulders moved in brief acknowledgement and

she turned her attention to Rosie. The little girl wasn't saying very much—in fact, both children had been unusually quiet this morning. Perhaps she should have expected that, since it was their first day at a new school. They didn't know this neighbourhood very well as yet, and they'd had to adjust to so many changes of late that it was understandable if they were struggling to take everything on board.

'How about you, Rosie? Are you all right?'

Rosie nodded, her expression solemn, her grey eyes downcast. 'I'm okay.' She was two years younger than her brother, but in some ways she seemed a little more mature than him. It looked as though she was coping, but you could never tell.

'I'm sure you'll be fine, both of you.' Sarah tried to sound encouraging. 'I know it's not easy, starting at a new school mid-term, but I expect your teachers will introduce you to everybody and you'll soon make friends.' She hesitated for a moment, but when neither child said anything in response she put an arm around each of them and started down the path towards the classrooms. 'Let's get you settled in—remember, if I'm still at work by the time school finishes, Murray from next door will come and pick you up.'

A few minutes later, she kissed them goodbye and left them in their cloakrooms, anxiety weighing heavily on her, but there was relief, too, when she saw that the other children were curious about the newcomers and had begun to talk to them.

Sarah pulled in a deep breath as she walked back to her car, trying to gather sustenance from an inner well of strength. It was difficult to know who felt worse, she or the children, but somehow she had to push those concerns to one side for the moment and get on with the rest of what looked to be a difficult day ahead.

It wasn't just the children who were suffering from first-day nerves—she would be starting out on a new job, riding along in the air ambulance with the immediate care doctor for the area. That would carry with it its own difficulties…but that wasn't what was troubling her. As a doctor herself, she hoped she was well prepared to cope with any medical emergency.

She set the car in motion, driving away from the small Cornish fishing village and heading along the coast road towards the air ambulance base where she was to meet up with James Benson.

Her hands tightened on the steering-wheel. Now, there was the crux of the problem. Even recalling his name caused a flurry of sensation to well up inside her abdomen and every now and again her stomach was doing strange, uncomfortable kinds of flip-overs.

How long had it been since she'd last seen him? A good many years, for sure… She'd been a teenager back then, naïve, innocent and desperate to have his attention. Her whole body flushed with heat at the memory, and she shook her head, as though that would push it away.

She'd do anything rather than have to meet up with him once again, but the chances of avoiding him had been scuppered from the outset. Maybe if she'd known from the start that he was a consultant in the emergency department where she'd wanted to work, she would never have applied for the post as a member of the team.

And how could she have known that he was also on

call with the air ambulance? It was a job she'd trained for, coveted, and once she'd been drawn in, hook, line and sinker, there was no way she could have backed out of the deal.

She drove swiftly, carefully, barely noticing that she had left the coast behind, with its spectacular cliffs and rugged inlets, and now she was passing through deeply wooded valleys with clusters of whitewashed stone cottages clinging to the hillsides here and there. The bluebells were in flower, presenting her with occasional glimpses of a soft carpet of blue amidst the undergrowth. Small, white pockets of wood sorrel peeped out from the hedges, vying for space with yellow vetch. It was beautiful, but she couldn't appreciate any of it while her heart ached from leaving the children behind and her nerves were stretched to breaking point from anticipating the meeting ahead.

At the base, she drove into a slot in the staff car park and then made her way into the building, to where the air ambulance personnel had their office. Bracing herself, she knocked briskly on the door and then went inside.

The room was empty and she frowned. She couldn't have missed a callout because the helicopter was standing outside on the helipad.

She took a moment to look around. There were various types of medical equipment on charge in here, a computer monitor displaying a log of the air ambulance's last few missions, and a red phone rested in a prominent position on the polished wooden desk. To one side of the room there was a worktop, where a kettle was making a gentle hissing sound as the water inside heated up.

'Ah, there you are.' She turned as James Benson's voice alerted her to his presence. Her heart began to race, pounding as those familiar, deep tones smoothed over her like melting, dark chocolate. 'I'm sorry I wasn't here to greet you,' he added. 'We've all been changing into our flight suits and generally getting ready for the off.'

She nodded, not trusting herself to speak just then. He was every bit as striking as she remembered, with that compelling presence that made you feel as though he dominated the room. Or perhaps it was just that she was unusually on edge today. He was tall, with a strong, muscular build, and he still had those dark good looks which, to her everlasting shame, had been her undoing all those years ago, the chiselled, angular bone structure and jet-black hair, and those penetrating grey eyes that homed in on you and missed nothing.

He was looking at her now, his thoughtful gaze moving over her, lighting on the long, burnished chestnut of her hair and coming to rest on the pale oval of her face.

'I wasn't sure if it really would be you,' he said. 'When I saw your name on the acceptance letter I wondered for a minute or two whether it might be some other Sarah Franklyn, but the chances of there being two doctors in the neighbourhood with the same name was pretty remote. I know you went to medical school and worked in Devon.' His glance meshed with hers, and she steeled herself not to look away. He'd obviously heard, from time to time, about what she was doing. She straightened her shoulders. She would get through this. Of course she would. How bad could it be?

'I expect my taking up a medical career seems a strange choice to you, knowing me from back then.' Her voice was husky, and she cleared her throat and tried again, aiming to sound more confident this time. 'You weren't in on the interviews, so it didn't occur to me that we would be working together.'

He inclined his head briefly. 'I was away, attending a conference—it was important and couldn't be avoided or delegated, so the head of Emergency made the final decision.' His mouth twisted in a way that suggested he wasn't too pleased about that, and Sarah felt a sudden surge of panic rise up to constrict her throat. So he didn't want her here. That was something she hadn't reckoned on.

His glance shifted slowly over her taut features and she lifted her chin in a brash attempt at keeping her poise.

His grey eyes darkened, but his voice remained steady and even toned. 'Perhaps you'd like to go and change into your flight suit, and then I'll show you around and introduce you to the rest of the crew. We'll have coffee. The kettle should have boiled by the time you're ready.'

'Yes. That sounds good.'

At least he was accepting her presence here as a done thing. That was a small mercy. And it looked as though he wasn't going to comment on what had happened all those years ago. Just the thought of him doing that was enough to twist her stomach into knots, but for now perhaps she was safe. After all, she'd been a vulnerable seventeen-year-old back then, and now, some nine years later, she was a grown woman who ought to be in full control of herself. Why, then, did she feel so ill at ease, so uncertain about everything?

But she knew the answer, didn't she? It was because, sooner or later, the past was bound to come up and haunt her.

He showed her to a room where she could change into her high-visibility, orange flight suit, and she took those few minutes of privacy to try and get herself together. She'd keep things on a professional level between them, nothing more, no private stuff to mess things up. That way, she could keep a tight grip on her emotions and show him that she was a totally different person now, calm and up to the mark, and nothing like she'd been as a teenager.

She cringed as she thought back to some of the things she had done in her early teen years. Had she really driven Ben Huxley's tractor around the village on that late summer evening? He'd forever regretted leaving the keys in the ignition, and his shock at discovering his beloved tractor stranded at a precarious angle in a ditch an hour later had been nothing to the concern he'd felt at finding a thirteen-year-old girl slumped over the wheel.

And what had been James's reaction when she'd broken into the stables on his father's estate one evening and saddled up one of the horses? It had been her fourteenth birthday and she hadn't cared a jot about what might happen or considered that what she had been doing was wrong. She had loved the horses, had been used to being around them, and on that day she'd felt an overwhelming need to ride through the meadows and somehow leave her troubles behind. She had been wild, reckless, completely out of control, and James had recognised that.

'None of this will bring your mother back,' he'd said to her, and she'd stared at him, her green eyes wide with defiance, her jaw lifted in challenge.

'What would you know about it?' she'd responded in a dismissive, careless tone.

She'd been extremely lucky. No one had reported her to the police. She'd got away with things, and yet the more she'd avoided paying for her misdemeanours, the more she'd played up. 'Mayhem in such a small package,' was the way James had put it. No wonder he didn't want her around now.

He made coffee for her when she went back into the main room a short time later. 'Is it still cream with one sugar?' he asked, and she gave him a bemused look, her mouth dropping open a little in surprise. He remembered that?

'Yes...please,' she said, and he waved her to a seat by the table.

'Tom is our pilot,' he said, nodding towards the man who sat beside her. Tom was in his forties, she guessed, black haired, with a smattering of grey streaks starting at his temples.

'Pleased to meet you, Sarah,' Tom said, smiling and pushing forward a platter filled with a selection of toasted sandwiches, which she guessed had been heated up in the mini-grill that stood on the worktop next to the coffee-maker. 'Help yourself. You never know if you're going to get a lunch break in this line of work, so you may as well eat while you get the chance.'

'Thanks.' She chose a bacon and cheese baguette and thought back to breakfast-time when she'd grabbed a slice of toast for herself while the children had tucked into their morning cereal. It seemed a long while ago now.

'And this is Alex, the co-pilot,' James said, turning to introduce the man opposite. He was somewhere in his mid-thirties, with wavy brown hair and friendly hazel eyes.

'Have you been up in a helicopter before?' Alex asked, and Sarah nodded.

'I worked with the air ambulance in Devon for a short time,' she answered. 'This is something I've wanted to do for quite a while, so when this job came up it looked like the ideal thing for me.'

He nodded. 'James told us you'll be working part time—is that by choice? It suits us, because our paramedic is employed on a part-time basis, too.'

'Yes. I'll just be doing one day a week here, and the rest of the time I'll be working at the hospital in the A and E department.'

'Sounds good. You'll get the best of both worlds, so to speak. It's unusual to do that, though, in A and E, I imagine?'

'Not so much these days,' Sarah murmured. 'And it suits me to do things this way.' She bit into her baguette and savoured the taste of melted cheese.

'Sarah supplements her income by doing internet work,' James put in. 'She writes a medical advice column for a website, and one for a newspaper, too.'

How had he known that? She looked up at him in surprise, and his mouth made a wry shape. 'I came across your advice column when I was browsing one day, and there was mention there of your work for the newspaper.' He frowned. 'I'm not sure it's wise to make diagnoses without seeing the patient.'

'That isn't what I do, as I'm sure you're aware if you've read my columns.' Perhaps he was testing her, playing devil's advocate, to see what kind of a doctor she really was, but she wasn't going to let him get away with implying she might not be up to the job. Neither was she going to tell him about her personal circumstances and give him further reason for doubting her suitability for the post. She needed to work part time so that she could be there for Sam and Rosie whenever possible, and the writing had provided an excellent solution in that respect. Working from home was a good compromise.

'I mostly work with a team of doctors,' she said, 'and we pick out letters from people who have conditions that would be of interest to a lot of others. We give the best advice we can in the circumstances, and point out other possible diagnoses and remedies.'

'Hmm. You don't think the best advice would be for your correspondents to go and see their own GP, or ask to see a specialist?'

'I think a good many people have already done that and are still confused. Besides, patients are much better informed these days. They like to visit the doctor with some inkling of what his responses might be, or what treatment options might be available to them,' she responded calmly.

He nodded. 'I guess you could be right.' He might have said more, but the red phone started to ring and he lifted the receiver without hesitation. He listened for a while and then said, 'What's the location? And his condition? Okay. We're on our way.'

Food and coffee were abandoned as they hurried out to the helicopter. 'A young man has been injured in a multiple-collision road-traffic accident,' James told them. 'He has a broken leg, but he's some thirty miles away from here, and the paramedics on scene feel they need a doctor present. He needs to go to hospital as soon as possible.'

They were airborne within a minute or two, and soon Sarah was gazing down at lush green fields bordering a sparse network of ribbon-like roads. James sat next to her, commenting briefly on the landmarks they flew over.

'There's the hospital,' he said, pointing out the helipad on top of the building. 'We'll be landing there when we have our patient secured.'

A little further on, they passed over a sprawling country estate, which had at its centre a large house built from grey, Cornish stone. It was an imposing, rectangular building, with lots of narrow, Georgian windows.

'Your family's place,' Sarah mused. 'Do you still live there?' It was large enough for him to have the whole of the north wing to himself. That's how things had been when she'd lived in the area, though he'd been away at medical school a good deal of the time, or working away at the hospital in Penzance. His younger brother had taken over the east wing, leaving the rest of the house to their parents.

He shook his head. 'I have my own place now. It

seemed for the best once I settled for working permanently in Truro. It's closer to the hospital. Jonathan still lives on the estate, though he has a family of his own now. He has a boy and a girl.'

'I wondered if he might stay on. He was always happy to live and work on the family farm, wasn't he?'

James nodded. 'So you decided to come back to your roots. What persuaded you to leave Devon? I have friends who worked there from time to time and, from what I heard on the grapevine, you were pretty much settled there. Rumour had it your mind was set on staying with the trauma unit.'

'That's pretty much the way it was to begin with… I was hoping I might get a permanent staff job but then I was passed over for promotion—a young male doctor pipped me at the post, and after that I started to look around for something else.'

He winced. 'That must have hurt.' He studied her briefly. 'Knowing you, I guess his appointment must have made you restless. You wouldn't have let the grass grow under your feet after that.'

'No, I wouldn't, that's true.' She wasn't going to tell him about her situation—although it hadn't been voiced at the time, she was fairly certain that she'd lost the promotion because of her family ties, and now she had to do everything she could to find secure, permanent work. This job promised all of that, but she was on three months' probation to see how things worked out on both sides, and she didn't need him to go looking for excuses to be rid of her before she signed a final contract.

By now they had reached their destination, and as the pilot came in to land, she could see the wreckage below. It looked as though a couple of motorcyclists had been involved in a collision with a saloon and a four-wheel-drive vehicle, and there were a number of casualties. A fire crew was in attendance, and from the blackened appearance of the saloon, it seemed that a blaze had erupted at some point. She could only hope the occupants of the car had escaped before the fire had taken hold.

'You'll be shadowing me,' James said, unclipping his seat belt as the helicopter came to a standstill, 'so don't worry about getting involved with the other patients. We'll take them in strict order of triage.'

Sarah bit her lip. She had no objection to following his lead and learning the ins and outs of this particular job, but surely she'd be of more use helping with the other victims of the crash?

'Okay, whatever you say. Though I do feel I could be of help with the rest of the injured.'

He was already on his way to the door of the helicopter, his medical kit strapped to his back in readiness. 'Let's see how it goes, shall we? According to the paramedics, our primary patient is in a bad way. He needs to be our main concern right now.'

Sarah followed him to the side of the road where a paramedic was tending an injured youth. There were police vehicles nearby and a young officer was directing traffic while another was setting up a road block.

She knelt down beside the casualty. He couldn't be much more than eighteen years old. He lay on the grass verge, well away from the traffic, and his face was white, blanched by shock and loss of blood. The paramedic was giving him oxygen through a mask.

'There are two people suffering from whiplash and sprains,' the paramedic told them. 'They're being looked after by my colleague, along with another man who has chest injuries—broken ribs and collarbone, from what we can tell so far. This lad is Daniel Henderson, motorcyclist. He and his friend were on their way to the coast when they ran into trouble. The two motor vehicles crashed at a road junction and the lads had no way of avoiding them.'

James was already assessing the extent of the boy's injuries. 'His lower leg's grossly deformed,' he said in a quiet voice. 'It looks like a fracture of both the tibia and fibula. That degree of distortion has to be affecting the blood supply.'

The paramedic nodded. 'He's in severe pain, he's very cold and his circulation is shutting down. We can't give him pain relief because we can't find a vein.'

It was a bad situation, because if there was an inadequate supply of blood to Daniel's foot there was the possibility that gangrene would set in and he might lose his leg.

'Thanks, Colin. I'll do an intraosseous injection,' James said, reaching into his medical bag for a bone injection gun. He spoke directly to the boy. 'I'm going to give you something to take away the pain, Daniel. It's a strong anaesthetic, so after a minute or two you'll be feeling much better. There'll be a sharp sting and soon after that you'll start to feel drowsy. Are you okay with that?'

Daniel nodded and closed his eyes. It was a case of the sooner the better, as far as he was concerned.

'Shall I clean the injection site and prepare the ketamine for you?' Sarah asked, and James nodded.

'Yes, thanks.'

As soon as she had cleaned and draped an area on Daniel's upper arm, James located the injection site and pressed the device on the gun that would insert a trocar through the bone and into the soft marrow that was filled with blood vessels. Once he'd done that, he removed the trocar and taped the cannula, the small-bore tube, in place.

Sarah connected an intravenous tube to the cannula and then James was able to give the boy the medication he needed. 'How are you doing, Daniel?' he asked softly after a while. 'Are you okay?'

'I'm all right.' Daniel's voice became slurred as the drug began to take effect.

'Can you feel this?' James pressed a wooden tongue depressor against his leg.

Daniel shook his head.

'That's good, it means the anaesthetic's working,' James said. He glanced at Sarah. 'I think we can safely try to realign the bones enough to restore his circulation. If you and Colin hold him still—Colin at his chest, and you, Sarah, take hold of his upper leg—I'll manoeuvre his ankle and start to pull. We'll need to take great care—we don't know how much damage has already been done to the blood vessels. Let's hope we can do this without too much of a struggle.'

He spoke softly so as not to alarm his patient, but Daniel was by now well anaesthetised and wasn't much concerned about what was happening. Sarah guessed he was simply glad to be free of pain at last.

James worked carefully to straighten out the broken bones as best he could, and as soon as he had achieved that to his satisfaction, he began to splint the leg to prevent any further movement.

'That should do the trick,' he said. 'His circulation should be restored now.'

Sarah kept an eye on Daniel the whole time. She was worried about him. He wasn't saying anything, and had appeared to be drifting in and out of consciousness throughout the procedure.

'We should put in a fluid line,' she said in an undertone. 'He's lost a lot of blood.'

'Yes,' James answered. 'Do you want to see to that, and then we'll transfer him to a spinal board?'

She didn't waste any time, and as soon as she had set up the line they worked together to make sure the young lad was comfortable and covered with a space blanket. Then they secured him with straps to the board so that he could be transferred to the helicopter.

James left them briefly while he went to check on the other patients, but he returned quickly and took his place beside Sarah in the helicopter.

'The others will be okay to travel by road,' he said. 'It'll take around an hour for them to get to the hospital, but they're in no immediate danger.'

He glanced at his patient. 'I've asked Tom to radio ahead and alert A and E to have an orthopaedic surgeon standing by,' he told Sarah. 'How's the lad doing?'

'His blood pressure's low and his heart rate is rapid, with a weak pulse,' she answered. The signs of shock were all there, but they'd done everything they could for now, and all they could do was wait.

Tom was already setting the helicopter in motion, lifting them up off the ground. Within minutes he had turned them around and they were heading out across the Cornish peninsula towards the hospital, some thirty miles away.

James checked on the injured youth, lifting the blanket to look at his feet. 'His toes are beginning to pink up,' he pointed out, glancing at Sarah.

'Oh, thank heaven,' she said. She smiled at him, her mouth curving, her green eyes bright with relief. With his circulation restored, the imminent danger of Daniel losing his leg had been averted. 'I'm so glad for him.'

James nodded. He gently tucked the blanket in place, but he didn't once take his gaze from Sarah. He was watching her closely, as though he was mesmerised, taking in the warmth of her response, the soft flush of heat that flared in her cheeks.

The breath caught in her throat, and a familiar hunger surged inside her as she returned his gaze. There was a sudden, dull ache in her chest, an ache that came from knowing her unbidden yearning could never be assuaged. He still had the power to melt her bones and fill her with that humiliating need that would forever be her downfall.

She closed her eyes briefly. How on earth would she be able to work with him over the weeks, months that lay ahead?

'We'll be coming in to land in about two minutes.' The pilot's voice came over the speaker.

'Okay, Tom. We'll be ready.' James turned his attention back to the boy on the stretcher. He was self-contained, in control, as always.

Sarah looked out of the window. She had to keep things between them on a professional footing. That was the only way she could survive. From now on it would become her mantra.

CHAPTER TWO

'You look as though you could do with a break. Has it been a tough week?' Murray laid a manila folder down on a corner of the pine kitchen table, avoiding the clutter of pastry boards and rolling pins. 'I brought the colour charts I promised you,' he added, tapping the folder. He stared at her, looking her up and down. 'You're not your usual jaunty self today. What's up?'

'Nothing's up.' Sarah smiled at her spiky-haired neighbour and waved him towards a chair. Perhaps she was a bit pale from being cooped up in the house, and since she was cooking with the children today there were probably traces of flour in her hair where she'd pushed it off her face with the back of her hand. 'If I look less than on top of the world, I guess it's because I was up till all hours last night, painting the walls in the living room. Sit down and I'll pour you some tea. We were just about to have a cup.'

'Sarah's going to paint our bedrooms next,' Sam put in eagerly. He was using a cutter to make gingerbread shapes, and he paused now to assess his handiwork. 'She said we can choose the colours—'cept for black. She won't let me have that.' His bottom lip jutted and he frowned as he thought about that for a second or two.

Then his eyes lit up. 'Purple would be good, though—or bright red.'

'We helped Sarah with the living room,' Rosie put in. 'Well, I did. Sam kept going off and playing on his game machine.' She looked at her older brother and shook her head.

'You were both a great help, all the same,' Sarah said, her eyes crinkling at the corners. 'It's going to be a long job, though,' she admitted, glancing at Murray as she went over to the worktop at the side of the room. She lifted up the sunshine-yellow teapot. 'I knew there would be a lot of work when we moved in here a fortnight ago. This place was in a pretty wretched state when I bought it.'

Murray pulled a face. 'I guessed it was bad—the old man who used to live here wasn't able to do much in the way of maintenance—but I knew he was looking for a quick sale once he'd decided to go and live with his son and his family in Somerset. I did what I could to help him out with things, but there was a limit to what I could do, with company business getting in the way. There were orders for goods coming in thick and fast and supplies from the warehouses were delayed and so on. There's been a lot to sort out over the last few months.' He frowned. 'Perhaps I shouldn't have pointed the house out to you,' he finished on a thoughtful note.

She poured his tea and came towards him once more, placing the mug in front of him. 'You did the right thing,' she told him, laying a hand on his shoulder and squeezing gently. 'I'm really glad you told me about this place. I don't know what I'd have done otherwise. It was exactly what I needed.'

'Hmm… Well, I suppose a lick of paint here and there will work wonders.' He glanced at the children, busy laying out gingerbread men on a baking tray. Rosie's were perfectly symmetrical, with raisins placed in exactly the right place to represent eyes. Sam, on the other hand, was far more slapdash in his approach, and his men looked like cross-eyed vagabonds, with bits missing here and there. Sarah suspected he'd been surreptitiously tasting the uncooked mixture every now and again—the greasy smears around his mouth were a dead give-away.

Murray looked at Sarah once more as she placed the first batch of gingerbread men in the hot oven. 'How's the job going? Is it working out for you?'

She sat in a chair opposite him, leaving it to the children to finish rolling out the remains of the gingerbread mix on a pastry board.

'I think so. It's early days yet. My boss is watching my every move.' She gave a wry smile. 'I think he's worried I might slip up and inadvertently kill off one of our patients.'

James had not made it obvious that he was concerned about her ability to make the grade, but for the last week he'd checked everything she did, going over her charts and medication logs with a keen eye. Every now and again she would be aware of him assessing her actions, scrutinising the way she handled various procedures. She'd no idea why he was concerned about her abilities as a doctor, but in the past she'd always been headstrong and haphazard in her actions, and maybe he thought she'd breezed her way through medical school on a wing and a prayer.

Murray laughed. 'As if!' Then he sobered, glancing at the children, and added in an undertone, 'Seriously, though, are you finding it all a bit much? You have a whole lot on your plate these days.'

'It's okay. I'm beginning to get used to the new routine. It's just that...' She broke off, her expression rueful. 'I don't know,' she said, after a moment or two. 'I don't seem to have time to sit and think at the moment. Everything seems to be going at a breakneck pace—moving in here, the new job, finding a school for the children, taking on the internet work. It's all come about in a short space of time.' She straightened up and sipped at her tea. 'I'm sure things will sort themselves out, though. Like I said, these are early days.'

'Maybe it would help if I took the kids out for a while. That would give you some time to yourself—unless you'd like to come with us?' He gave her a thoughtful look. 'I need to head into town to pick up some hardware for my computer and I thought about dropping into the pizza place while I'm in the area.'

Sam's ears pricked up at the mention of pizza. 'When are you going? Can I go with you?'

'Sure.' Murray laughed. 'If Sarah thinks it's okay, that is.' He glanced at her and she nodded. She'd known Murray for years, ever since they'd both taken part in a rock-climbing course at an outdoor pursuits centre. He ran his own internet company, working from home most of the time, selling sports equipment and accessories, advising people on how to keep fit, and setting up weekend sporting activities. She'd always found him to be reliable and trustworthy. The children would be safe with him, that was for sure.

'That's fine with me. I think I'll give it a miss, though, if you don't mind. I think I need some time to get myself together.' It had been a stressful week, one way and another, and being with James every day had been harder to handle than she'd expected. She'd always known she should keep her distance from him, but now that she'd taken the job that was never going to happen. Every instinct warned her that whatever way she became involved with him, she might end up being hurt. He alone had the power to affect her that way. Emotionally he could leave her bereft.

She dragged her mind back to Murray's offer. 'I have to go and buy some groceries from the village store, and I could do with a walk along the clifftop and maybe even along the beach.' She smiled. 'Rosie and Sam never seem quite as keen on doing that as I am.'

Murray nodded and turned to look at Rosie. 'How does pizza sound to you, Rosie? Are you in?'

'Yes, please.' She looked at Sarah and said hesitantly, 'I don't mind going for walks…not really… It's just that…' She broke off, her shoulders wriggling. 'Mum used to take us along the seafront in Devon. Now… I get… I get all sad now when we go to the beach.' Her eyes were downcast, and her lower lip was beginning to tremble.

'Oh, Rosie…' Sarah's heart swelled with compassion, and she quickly stood up and went over to her. 'I know how you must be feeling, pumpkin.' She put her arms around the little girl and held her close. 'I do understand. It's hard…but you'll see, it'll get easier with time.'

'We used to play football on the beach with Dad sometimes,' Sam said, a wistful, far-away look in his blue-grey eyes. 'He used to dive for the ball and then he'd fall over and we'd wrestle him for it.'

Sarah reached out and gently stroked his hair. She didn't remember her father ever playing rough-and-tumble games like that with her when she'd been younger, but obviously he had changed, grasping a second chance of happiness after he had found her stepmother and started his new family. She felt for Rosie and Sam. They were going through something that no child should ever have to bear, but she was doing whatever she could to make life easier for them. It was difficult, though, because memories would come flooding in at unexpected moments, like this, putting her on the spot.

'Sounds as though you could all do with a bit of cheering up,' Murray said, coming to her rescue. 'I think pizza with all the toppings will probably do the trick—and we could take some of your game DVDs into the store and swap them for those you were telling me about, Sam, if you like?'

'Oh, yeah…that'd be great.' Sam's mood changed in mercurial fashion.

'Rosie, you might like to check out some of the dance games,' Sarah suggested, following Murray's lead. 'You have some pocket money saved up, don't you?'

Rosie brightened and nodded, causing her soft brown curls to flutter and gleam in the sunlight that poured in through the kitchen window.

'That's settled, then,' Murray said. 'As soon as you're ready, we'll be off.'

After they had gone, Sarah cleared away and set out the cooked gingerbread men on racks to cool. A few were missing already, since Murray and the children had decided they smelled too good to leave until later. Sam's pockets had been bulging as he'd left the house.

She looked around, suddenly feeling the need to go out and get away from all the jobs that were crying out for attention. Sam and Rosie would be gone for much of the afternoon, according to Murray, so maybe she would make the most of things and go and get some fresh air. The walk into the centre of the village would do her good and she could pick up some fresh supplies from the grocery store while she was there.

It was a beautiful spring day, with a blue sky overhead and patchy white clouds moving in from the coast. As she walked down the hill towards the seafront, past colour-washed cottages and narrow, cobbled side streets, she could feel the light breeze lifting her hair and billowing gently round the hem of her skirt. In the distance, boats were moored in the harbour, and closer to home fishermen tended their nets, laying them out on the smooth sand as they looked them over and prepared for the next trip out to sea.

Instead of going directly down to the beach, she took a path that led to a raised terrace overlooking the cove, and from there she gazed out across the bay towards the craggy promontory she had once explored as a teenager. It was some distance away, but she could see the waves dashing against the rocks, sending up fountains of spray to splash into the crevices. She'd gone there once with friends, and James had joined them. He had been on one of his brief visits home from medical school. He'd walked with her along the shore as she'd looked for shells buried in the warm sand. It had been a magical day, with the sun high in the sky and James by her side, a day that had almost made her dreams come true.

There was a movement beside her and it was almost as though by thinking of him she'd conjured him up. 'It must seem a long time ago since you spent your days searching for crabs in those rock pools,' James said, coming out of the blue to stand alongside her. He followed her gaze to the boulder-strewn beach some half a mile away.

She gave a startled jump, taking a step backwards as he went to place a hand on the metal railing in front of them. He quickly put his arm out to steady her, and then when she'd recovered her balance he let his hand rest on the curve of her hip.

'Are you all right? I'm sorry if I surprised you.' He sounded concerned and his glance moved over her to gauge her reaction. 'I didn't mean to creep up on you like that. I thought you'd be aware of me, but you must have been miles away in your head.'

'Yes... I'm okay.' She rested her fingers against her chest, on the soft cotton of her top, as though that might somehow calm the staccato beat of her heart. Where had he come from? She couldn't think straight while he was so close, with his hand spreading fire along her skin, sending heated ripples of sensation to spread through her hips and along the length of her spine. 'What... what are you doing here? Where did you come from?'

'I was on my way home from the hospital and I decided to stop and pick up something to snack on from the village shop. Then I saw you standing here.'

'Oh, I see.' She frowned. 'I thought this was your weekend off.'

He removed his hand and stepped closer to the rail, turning so that he could look at her properly. That ought to have made things easier for her, but instead her mind went blank for a moment or two as she unexpectedly felt the loss of his warm, intimate touch. Perversely, she wanted him to go on holding her.

'Yes, it is, but one of the junior doctors was anxious about a patient and phoned me to ask what he should do. Apparently the consultant in charge was busy dealing with another emergency.'

'Were you all right with that?' She'd watched him work hard all week, putting in long hours, staying on to make sure his patients pulled through and were definitely stabilised or on the road to recovery before he would leave. He seemed reluctant to hand over responsibility until he had done everything humanly possible to make sure they were safe. It must have taken a toll on him, but it didn't show. Despite all that supreme effort, he still managed to look fit and energetic, on top form.

Weekends were precious for everyone, but some senior medical staff guarded them as sacrosanct, a time to recuperate and recharge their batteries, something they'd earned after years of study and acquiring specialist qualifications. From what she'd heard, one or two consultants took a very dim view of things if juniors called them in to work out of hours. Of course, things tended to operate differently in the emergency department.

'I was fine with it,' James said. 'I'd sooner I was there to see a patient if there are any worries about his or her condition. Junior doctors do their best, but they need support, and I try to give it as much as possible.

Sometimes you can do it over the phone, but other times there's nothing for it but to go in.'

'Yes, of course.' She had finished her foundation years, but she wasn't much more than a junior doctor herself—James was far more experienced than she was. He'd started his training while she'd been about to begin her worrisome teens, and he'd always put his heart and soul into medicine. 'What was the problem with the patient?' She might be in the same boat herself one day, in a quandary as to whether she should call him out, and it would be helpful to know what kind of things she ought to bring to his attention.

'A woman collapsed while she was being treated for an abdominal injury. The doctor followed all the protocols but she wasn't responding, so in the end he called me to ask for advice. The senior staff were all too busy with other emergencies. There was obviously something more going on than the problems with her injury, but her medical records weren't available. Her liver was damaged, nothing too major—at least, not enough to cause her total collapse. I've ordered a batch of tests, so we'll know better what's going on as soon as they come back from the lab. She's being given supportive treatment in the meantime.'

His glance wandered over her, taking in the pale-coloured cotton top that faithfully followed her curves, and the gently flowing skirt that skimmed her hips, drifting and settling around her calves as she moved. His grey eyes seemed to glimmer as he studied her, though of course it might simply have been a trick of the light. 'You're looking very summery...just right for this warm sunshine,' he said.

A wave of heat surged through her. She hadn't expected him to comment or even notice how she looked, but perhaps it was the contrast between how she looked now and the way she dressed at work that had sparked his interest. One day a week when she went out with the air ambulance, when she wore a flight suit, and the rest of the time at work she dressed in scrubs, the basic A and E outfit.

She gave a wry smile. 'It beats wearing scrubs, anyway, or even jeans. Just lately, when I'm at home I've been trying to get on with some decorating any chance I get, so it makes a change to be out of jeans for a while.'

'Ah…of course, you only moved back here a couple of weeks ago, didn't you? I imagine there's a lot to do, settling into a new place.'

'Yes, you're right there. My back certainly knows all about it.' She laughed, rubbing a hand over muscles that had only recently made themselves known to her.

'Perhaps it's just as well you're having the afternoon off, then. Are you taking some time off from the decorating to explore the village? I expect you want to get to know the place all over again.' He leaned back against the rail, at ease, his long body thoroughly relaxed as he watched her.

'Yes, I thought I'd wander around for a while. Though, like you, I need to get some supplies from the store. I did a big shop when we arrived but now I'm running out of a few things.'

She glanced at him. He was smartly dressed, in dark, clean-cut trousers and a deep blue shirt, the kind of thing he usually wore for work in the emergency unit when he wasn't in scrubs. Perhaps he'd left his jacket in his car, along with his tie. His shirt was open at the neck, exposing an area of smooth, suntanned throat. She looked away. 'Did you park up somewhere around here?' she asked.

He nodded. 'By the quayside. I don't live too far away from here, but it's more than a short walk and it's uphill all the way.' He pointed to the steps that were built into the hillside, with a protective rail to help along the way.

Sarah glanced at the steep, green slopes, covered with a rich array of grasses and shrubs. At intervals there were houses dotted about, overlooking the sea. 'Do you live in one of those?' she asked.

'No. You can't see my house from here. It's further back, about a mile inland. I walk to the village sometimes to stretch my legs and take in the scenery.'

'It must be a big change for you after all those years of living on your parents' country estate.'

'Yes, it is. But I like having my own space.' He looked out to sea for a while, and they both watched a sailing vessel move across the horizon. 'I wondered if you'd ever come back to Cornwall,' he said. 'You were in Devon for several years, weren't you? Did you stay with your father there? He'd remarried before you left here, hadn't he?'

'Yes, he had…and Sam was already a year old by then. I did stay with my father in Devon for a short time.' She moved restlessly, uncomfortable with memories that crowded her brain, and he followed as she began to walk along the cliff path.

'But then…?'

'I began to wonder if I might be in the way. What

newly married couple wants a teenager around?' She pulled a face. 'Anyway, it wasn't long before I went away to medical school, and I was glad to be independent. And it was easier to rent my own place, once I found friends to share with me.'

'How did your father feel about that? After all, you and he had quite a few years here in Cornwall when it was just the two of you together.'

She shrugged awkwardly. 'It was never all that comfortable for either of us once we were left on our own. He was withdrawn a lot of the time, and he preferred to be by himself. He'd have cut himself off from everyone and everything if it had been possible, but instead he had to go out to work to keep a roof over our heads. Then he met Tracy and everything changed.'

He frowned, looking at her with an intent expression. 'That must have been hard on you after all that time of being out in the cold, so to speak.'

She pressed her lips together briefly. 'She obviously sparked something in him that gave him a renewed zest for life. I guess I was glad he'd found some reason to join the human race once more.' The path led down from where they were to the centre of the village, where the grocery store and the post office stood side by side. 'I need to buy some fresh vegetables and a loaf of bread,' she announced. 'Are you heading in the same direction as me?'

'I am. I thought I might get some sticky buns and one of Martha's hot coffees to take away.' He sent her a quick glance. 'Perhaps you'd like to help me eat them— I didn't have breakfast and I missed out on lunch with being called out so early this morning. It's lazy of me,

I know, but I can't be bothered to go back home and cook.'

Her green eyes widened a fraction. 'It's the middle of the afternoon,' she said in astonishment. 'You ought to know better than to go without food in our line of work.'

He nodded, his mouth making a crooked line. His whole countenance changed when he smiled, and her heart gave a small lurch. 'Consider me told off,' he said. 'How about the buns? Do you want to share?'

'Okay.' She pushed open the door of the shop and a bell jangled to alert Martha, the proprietor, to her customers. 'But I'll go one better than that. Why don't you come over to my place and I'll heat up some soup and warm some bread rolls in the oven? Then you can have the buns for afters. I only live about five minutes' walk from here.' The suggestion was out before she had time to consider whether she was wise to get in closer contact with this man who had haunted her, metaphorically speaking, ever since her change from teenage brat to emerging womanhood.

'Well, that's too good an offer to miss...if you're sure?' His brow creased. 'I don't want to put you to any trouble.'

'It's no bother. But if you were to collapse through malnutrition, I wouldn't want to have it on my conscience.' She gave him an admonishing glance and he laughed.

'Thanks, Sarah. Besides, I'm curious to see where you're living now. I heard you'd bought a place, rather than renting. That sounds enterprising, coming from a girl who wanted to be free as a bird and explore new pastures.'

'Hmm.' Her cheeks flushed with warm colour. 'I was very young and naïve when I came out with that statement.' She'd been brash, full of youthful defiance, keen to let him know that she wouldn't be staying around for much longer. In truth, in her mind, she'd been running away. Her mouth made an odd twist. 'It's actually not up to much, and I think you might be quite disappointed when you see it. I know I was, but I was already contracted to buy it.'

He gave her a perplexed glance. 'You mean you bought it without seeing it?'

'That's right. It came up for auction and I didn't have time to suss it out before putting in an offer. It was just about as much as I could afford.' She lifted her arms in a futile gesture. 'And I was in a bit of a hurry.'

'It sounds like it.'

'Can I help you?' Martha bustled forward, ready to serve them, her face creasing in a smile. 'Have you managed to sort yourself out, my dear?' she queried gently, looking at Sarah. 'You did quite a bit of stocking up last time you were in here, didn't you? I must say, you don't look quite as harassed as you did then.'

'I think it's all beginning to work out,' Sarah answered cheerfully. 'You had pretty well everything I needed to get me started with the cleaning and so on… but I just want a few bits this time around.'

Martha collected together everything off Sarah's list, and she and James left the shop a few minutes later, loaded with packages. James was munching on one of the buns he'd bought.

'Here, let me carry those for you,' he said, relieving her of a couple of bags. He peered inside them.

'There are a lot of vegetables in here for just one young woman.'

'Ah…perhaps you didn't know…' She sent him a quick, sideways look. 'I'm not on my own these days.'

'You're not?' His step halted momentarily and he frowned, glancing at her ring finger and then, seeing that it was bare, said, 'Have I missed something? Are you involved with someone?'

'No, it's nothing like that.' She walked determinedly up the hill towards her cottage.

He sent her a puzzled look, but they'd reached her house by now and she stood still, looking up at the blotchy, white-painted building with its peeling wood-work. 'This is it. This is where I'm living now.'

He stared, his gaze moving up to the roof where a few slates were cracked or missing altogether. To his credit, he managed to keep a straight face as he said slowly, 'I think you might have your work cut out here.'

She laughed. 'You said it…but that's nothing. Wait till you see the inside.' She'd already reinforced his view that she was as reckless as ever, buying on impulse, so what did it matter if he looked around and saw the piti-ful state it was in?

They walked along the drab hallway to the kitchen, where he set the bags and packages down on the pine table. He glanced thoughtfully around the room for a moment or two, taking in the flaking ceiling and the windows that hadn't seen a lick of paint for quite some time.

'The cupboards and worktops look as though they're made of solid wood,' he commented after a while. 'I suppose they could be stripped back and restored to their original condition—or painted, depending on how you feel about it.'

'Hmm. Yes, you're right. I haven't quite decided what I'm going to do yet.' She smiled at him. He was being positive, and that made her feel much better. 'I'll put the soup on a low heat, and the rolls in the oven, and I could show you around the place while they're warming up, if you like?'

He nodded. 'Sounds good to me. Can I do anything to help? Shall I put the kettle on?'

'Okay, thanks. Mugs are over there, cutlery in the drawer.'

They worked together for a while, and then she took him on a whistle-stop tour of the three-bedroomed cottage, pointing out the best features, where she was able to find any.

'I knew the structure of the house was reasonably sound when I bid for it,' she told him, 'because Murray, my neighbour, is a good friend, and he knew about the property—from a layman's point of view, of course.'

'Ah...I see... I think.' He hesitated. 'Have you known him long?'

She nodded. 'For years, though of course we've been out of touch until recently. He's been a great help to me.' They were in one of the bedrooms, and she waved a hand towards the small fireplace. 'I'm not sure quite what to do about that. As you've seen, there's a fireplace in each of the three bedrooms.' She frowned. 'They say you should keep any character features like that if at all possible when you're renovating, but they don't look too good at the moment, and anyway I'm wondering if the rooms might be a bit chilly with the open chimney.'

He shook his head. 'The chimney shouldn't make any difference, and from the looks of things you have central heating, which should keep everything cosy. I think it would be a good idea to keep them. The house is Victorian and pretty solid in most respects, and it would be a pity to lose its character. It should be a fairly straightforward job to renovate them—you have to get rid of any rust, of course, apply a coat of red oxide and then when that's dry rub in some black grate polish. It doesn't come off once it's done, and the fireplace will look as good as new.'

'You're probably right.' She was thoughtful. 'I'll put it on my list of things to do——it's getting to be quite a long list.'

'I could do it for you, if you like.'

She blinked in astonishment. 'You'd do that?' She was completely bowled over by his unexpected offer. Why would he want to spend time doing anything at all in this old, neglected house? And why would he do it for her?

'I think it's something I would enjoy.' He went over to the fireplace and ran his fingers lightly over the partially engraved cast iron. 'I often did restoration work in the family home, don't you remember? There was that time I was up a stepladder, trying to decide what colours to use on the ornate ceiling in the dining room, when you walked in.' He sent her an oblique glance, a glimmer sparking in his dark eyes.

'Oh.' The breath left her lungs in a small gasp. How could he have brought that up? Did he recall everything, every tiny instance of when she'd brought havoc into his life? 'How was I to know you were balanced on a ladder?' she said. 'I didn't mean to take you by surprise. All I knew was I was supposed to go to the house and find someone who would get me started on the apple picking. I should have gone to the study, but I went into the dining room by mistake.'

'And I narrowly avoided taking a nose dive.'

'Because I managed to steady the ladder just in time—'

'Only after I grabbed hold of the mahogany cabinet and regained my balance.'

'Yes, well…' Sarah clamped her mouth shut. Perhaps it was for the best if she didn't say any more. It was an experience that had alarmed her greatly at the time. For a number of years she had worked on the estate in the summer holidays and this particular season she had been scheduled to spend time in the orchards. She hadn't meant to catch her employer's son off guard, and the consequences could have been disastrous. 'You made a good job of the ceiling anyway,' she said, breaking her vow of silence.

He grinned. 'I guess I did, in the end. It took a while, though. A couple of weeks at least.' He moved away from the fireplace. 'I'll make a start with the fires as soon as I get hold of the red oxide and the polish…that'll be sometime next week, I expect.'

'Um, okay. Thanks. That would be really good. I'm really stunned that you should offer.' She looked around for a moment at the fading wallpaper and gave a soft sigh. It would all get done eventually.

'As you say, the house is sound in most respects,' James commented, interpreting her rueful expression.

'It doesn't look much now, but with care and attention it could be something quite special.'

She smiled at him. 'Yes, you're right, of course.' She turned towards the door and said, 'I think you've seen everything now—shall we go and see if the soup's ready?'

The kitchen was warm from the old AGA, and Sarah soon had the table set for the meal. She put out butter, ham and cheese, along with a bowl of fresh salad, and invited James to sit and eat. Then she remembered the gingerbread men and laid some out on a plate, sliding it alongside the sticky buns James had bought.

'Help yourself,' she said, taking a seat across the table from him.

He smiled as he looked at the food, and sniffed the air appreciatively. 'Mmm,' he murmured, ladling soup from the tureen into his bowl. 'This smells appetising— like home-cooked vegetables in a rich, meaty broth.' He dipped his spoon in the soup and tasted the mixture, his eyes widening in surprise. 'Ah…this is wonderful. I don't think I've ever tasted anything quite like it.'

'Well, I'm glad to hear it—though if you're that hungry, I expect anything would taste good right now.' She grinned. 'Although I did spend a good deal of yesterday evening getting it ready.'

His dark brows rose, and he looked at her dubiously, as though he expected to see her nose grow like Pinocchio's had whenever he'd told a lie. 'You're kidding me,' he said in astonishment. 'You, spending time in a kitchen? I can scarcely believe it. As I recall, you'd sooner grab a burger or a baguette or stick something in the microwave so that you could be on your way. Wherever did you learn to cook?'

'Oh, here and there. It turned out to be a bit of a necessity once I was on my own.' She laughed. 'To be honest, I soon got very tired of convenience food and decided I needed to buy a cook book.' She helped herself to salad, adding grated cheese to her plate alongside the ham.

'You certainly look good on whatever it is you've been eating these last few years.' His glance trailed over her. 'You've filled out—as I recall, you were a skinny little thing with flyaway hair that was forever coming loose from the pins, or whatever it was you used to keep it in place.'

Her mouth made a brief, crooked slant. 'Not much change with the hair, then.' She'd brushed it before leaving the house, securing it in a topknot as best she could, and even now she could feel silky strands parting company with the clips.

She bent her head and pretended to be absorbed with her meal. He'd called her skinny. No wonder he'd not even looked at her the way she'd hoped for back then when she'd been seventeen. Warm colour filled her cheeks. Skinny. He'd made a twosome with Chloe, the daughter of the local innkeeper—she'd had curves aplenty, along with golden hair and dreamy blue eyes. She'd seen them having lunch together at a pub, and his defection had been the final straw to a love-starved teenager. She'd vowed then she would get away from the village and leave James far behind.

And yet now she was sharing a meal with him in her fading, love-starved cottage. She must be mad.

She gathered her composure and forced herself to look at him once more. 'I made another pot of tea—would you like a cup?' She was already reaching for the teapot.

He nodded. 'Thanks. That would be great.' He was staring absentmindedly at the plate of gingerbread men. Some had bits of leg missing, or half an arm, and that made him smile. 'They smell good—more wounded soldier than fighting men, I'd guess,' he said.

'Oh, yes. They're Sam's addition to the feast. He's always in too much of a hurry to bother with perfection.'

He frowned. 'Sam—so there's someone else, as well as Murray? Your life must be getting quite complicated.'

'Yes.' She glanced at him and said quietly, 'Perhaps you haven't heard what happened to my father and Tracy?' It had been a terrible shock, and she had never felt more alone in her life when she'd heard the news of their accident.

'Something happened to them?' His expression was suddenly serious, and Sarah nodded unhappily.

'They were caught up in a road-traffic accident.' She pressed her lips together briefly. 'Unfortunately their injuries were serious and they died almost instantly.'

He drew in a sharp breath, his features taut. 'I didn't know. I'm so sorry, Sarah. That must have been awful for you.'

'It was. It was a difficult time.' She closed her eyes fleetingly, resting a hand on the table, unable to concentrate on anything for that moment, while her mind was lost in the memory of those dreadful weeks when the world as she'd known it had come to a standstill.

His fingers closed over hers, in a comforting gesture

that brought her back to the present and made her look up into his dark eyes.

'Did you have friends to support you?'

'Thankfully, yes.'

'I'm glad. I wish I could have been there for you.'

'Thank you.' She sent him a gentle smile. 'But I coped. The biggest problem for me back then was what to do about Sam and Rosie, of course…my half-brother and half-sister. Sam's ten years old, and Rosie's eight.' She frowned. 'I think you might have seen Sam when he was a baby…at the wedding reception of a mutual friend. Anyway, they both live with me now.'

'But…surely there was some other relative who could have taken them in? An uncle and aunt, perhaps?' He looked shocked. 'How can it be that you're looking after them?'

Her shoulders lifted. 'There's no one else, so they're my responsibility now. That's why we moved back here, so that I could take up this new job and hopefully keep a roof over our heads.'

He shook his head, a perplexed expression on his face. 'I'd no idea, none at all.'

'Why would you?' she said quietly.

They finished their meal and James helped her to clear away. It was plain to see he was stunned by what she had told him, and later, when he was getting ready to leave, he said, 'You've taken on something that others would baulk at, you know.' His features relaxed. 'But somehow I might have expected it of you. You were always up for a challenge, weren't you?' His mouth twisted. 'Let's hope this one doesn't turn and bite back.'

CHAPTER THREE

'How are you feeling today, Nicola?' James picked up his patient's chart and then moved to the bedside where he gave the woman an engaging smile.

'So-so.' She tried to smile in return, but Sarah could see that she was extremely fatigued and clearly very unwell. Nicola Carter was in her mid-forties, with anxious grey eyes and brown hair that formed soft waves around her pale face. There was an intravenous drip connected to a cannula in her arm giving her lifesaving fluids. 'I feel a bit dizzy, and I keep being sick.'

'Mmm.' James nodded, showing his understanding and concern. 'It probably doesn't help that your blood pressure is very low. Your liver was bruised in the car crash and there was some bleeding inside your abdomen, which is why it is so important that you have complete bed-rest for a few days. You were in a bad way when you came into A and E on Saturday, and we still need to find out exactly what happened. It wasn't just the accident that caused you to collapse.' He glanced briefly at her notes. 'You haven't been eating much these last few months, have you? You've lost quite a bit of weight recently.'

'I just don't seem to have much of an appetite.'

'Well, we'll have to do something about that, and make sure we get you feeling better as soon as possible.' He laid a hand on hers. 'With any luck we should have the results of the latest tests by tomorrow. In the meantime, get as much rest as you can.'

'Okay.'

James moved away from the bedside, and Sarah followed. She'd gone with him each day on these rounds of the observation ward, and she was used by now to his gentle manner and matter-of-fact way of dealing with his patients. Somehow he managed to put them at ease so that they could feel reassured they were in good hands.

'I want you to follow up on Nicola's case,' he said now, replacing the chart in the slot at the end of the bed. 'With any luck, the internal bleeding will stop completely and she'll start to heal.'

'I'll see to it.'

'Good.' They walked together towards the A and E department, and he sent her an oblique glance, his grey eyes thoughtful. 'Thanks for giving me lunch the other day. I appreciated you taking the time and trouble to do that.' His mouth curved. 'And it was great to have the chance to look around your house.'

'Do you know—I enjoyed showing you? You actually helped me to see the place through fresh eyes.' She smiled. 'I wasn't sure what I was going to do about the children's bedrooms, how I was going to make them cosy and child-friendly, but you had some great ideas about using the old furniture in there. I'm going to spruce up the Victorian dressing screen and put it in Rosie's room—she'll find all sorts of ways to use it for imaginative games, I expect. And Sam will love to have the desk from the front room. He's really into drawing and writing these days.'

They left the observation ward and headed along the corridor, and James held open the fire door to let her pass through into the A and E department. 'I hadn't realised you'd taken on quite so much, with the children, especially. It must be difficult for you. I mean, you're so young, and you have your whole life ahead of you. Were there really no other options?'

Sarah shook her head. He wouldn't understand her reasoning because he was a bachelor, used to the freedom of his bachelor lifestyle. 'Even if there were, I wouldn't have taken them. I know what it's like to be left, to lose a parent, and they lost both of theirs. I wanted to smooth things for them, to show them that they still had family, someone who cared about them and who would be there for them.'

His mouth made a crooked slant. 'Given your background, I suppose I shouldn't have expected you to do anything else.'

'I guess so. Their situation is different from mine, of course, but they've had to put up with a lot, leaving their home behind, moving from Devon to Cornwall, settling into a new house and a new school. It's all happened quite fast, but I think they're beginning to make friends, so it should be a little easier for them from now on. I'm trying to involve them in the renovations as well, asking them for ideas and so on and giving them small jobs to do so that they feel they're part of it.' At least she could give them love and tenderness, things that had been sadly missing in her own early years.

'With your help, I'm sure they'll do all right. And doing up the house is a project that's going to keep all of you busy for the next few months.' He sent her a questioning glance. 'Speaking of which, I could come round this evening to make a start on the fireplaces, if you like...if that suits you?'

'That would be great, thanks.' It was good to know that he'd meant what he'd said about helping.

'I'm sure Sam will be happy with his new bedroom.' James chuckled. 'Didn't you say you're going to paint one of the walls red? Better that than the all-round black he was talking about.'

'I think he must be going through a Goth phase.' She laughed with him. 'I thought of compromising and doing a midnight blue ceiling with stars. I haven't made up my mind yet, though.'

'Who knows,' he said in an amused tone, 'if you encourage an interest in the stars and planets, he might grow up to be an astronomer.'

'Yeah, maybe. I wonder if they do astronaut suits in black?'

'Ah...there you are, James.' The triage nurse looked pleased to see him, and hurried towards them as they made their way to the central desk. 'I was just about to page you.' She paused to catch her breath. 'We've a young girl, Rachel, about seventeen years old, coming in by ambulance. She's been partying all weekend from the sound of things. It's a regular thing with her, apparently. She collapsed at a friend's house—they say she'd been drinking and experimenting with Ecstasy.'

James winced. 'We've been getting far too many of these cases lately. And they seem to be getting younger.'

He glanced briefly at the white board that detailed patients being treated in the emergency unit. 'Thanks, Gemma. We'll take her into the resuscitation room.'

'Okay. Do you want me to stand by?'

He shook his head. 'Sarah is shadowing me for these first few weeks, so she'll assist me on this one. I can see from the board that you have enough on your hands already.'

'Too right. It's been frantic here this morning from the outset.' Gemma walked swiftly away, leaving them to go and meet their young patient at the ambulance bay.

A paramedic was giving Rachel oxygen through a mask. 'She was talking at one stage—very upset and not making any sense, something about her family— but now she's unresponsive,' he told them. 'Her temperature's raised and her heart rhythm is chaotic. Blood pressure's high, too.'

By the time they had wheeled her into Resus, the girl had begun to have seizures, her whole body jerking in an uncoordinated fashion. James gave the teenager an injection of a benzodiazepine to control the convulsions while Sarah did a swift blood glucose test.

'She's hypoglycaemic,' she said, and James nodded.

'Give her dextrose, and thiamine to help with the alcohol problem. As soon as the seizure stops, we need to get in a fluid line.'

'Will do.' Sarah worked quickly to gain intravenous access. They both knew that the biggest danger to their patient right now was dehydration. Alcohol consumption caused loss of fluid volume due to increased urine output, and that could bring about problems with the heart and blood pressure and lead to collapse.

'I think it will be safer if we intubate her,' James said, gently introducing a short, flexible tube into the girl's windpipe and connecting it to a respirator. 'This way we can be sure she won't choke on her own vomit. And we need to get her temperature down.'

'I'll get the cool-air fan.' Sarah set that up and then paused for a moment to look down at the girl lying on the hospital bed. Her waif-like face was damp with perspiration so that her long brown hair clung to her cheeks and temples. She was dressed in party clothes, a skinny rib top and short skirt, with dark-coloured leggings that only emphasised her painfully thin frame.

'Apparently she talked about family,' she said quietly. 'From the notes, it looks as though Gemma hasn't been able to contact the parents yet. Perhaps I should talk to her friends and see what I can find out.'

'That's a good idea.' By now, James had set up the ECG machine to monitor the teenager's heart rhythm, and he had begun to write out the medication chart. 'I'm worried about the effect the alcohol and the Ecstasy are having on her heart,' he said, his mouth making a flat line. 'She's so young, and all this is such a waste.'

'They call it the love drug, don't they? It's supposed to make you feel warm and fuzzy and you want to hug everyone around you. Perhaps that was what she was looking for.'

'Maybe so, but she's ended up with a whole lot more that she didn't bargain for. If she comes out of this all right, she'll be a very lucky young woman.'

'I guess you're right. But perhaps we all do things we regret sometimes.'

He frowned, looking intently at her, his dark gaze searching her face.

She looked away, a rush of heat filling her cheeks. She didn't want to recall the things she'd done…especially that one time she'd had too much to drink…and she fervently hoped he'd forgotten it, that it hadn't made an impression on him. It had been as though she'd been determined to throw herself headlong into disaster. She shuddered, trying not to think about it. She wasn't the same person now.

She ran a hand through her long, silky, chestnut hair. 'I went a little crazy after my mother left. But I've had a lot of time to go over it in my mind.' She frowned. 'I think, all the time I was acting up, I was looking for something—something that would help me to make sense of my life and give me a reason to go on. After my mother walked out, I was hurt, desperately hurt, and bewildered more than anything else. I was sure I'd done something wrong, that I'd made her hate me so that she left me behind. I kept asking myself why else would she have done that. Didn't she know that I needed her? For a long, long time I went through a kind of grieving process.'

Her eyes clouded as she thought about those months, years of despair, and for a while she was silent, turning over the events of the past in her mind. Even now, she felt the bitter sting of that moment, watching her mother walk away, not knowing that was the last time she would ever see her—the revelation that she had gone from her life came later on, and it hit her as keenly now as if it had happened only yesterday.

'I'm sorry.' James placed the medicine chart on the

bed and reached for her, his hand lightly circling her arm. 'You were only twelve years old when she left. It's no wonder that you were devastated after she'd gone.'

He drew her away from the bedside. 'Let's go and get a cup of coffee, take a break for a while. We can go outside in the fresh air if you like.'

'I…I don't know. Are you okay with leaving Rachel?' They'd been on the go for the last two or three hours and she could do with a short break, but even so she glanced doubtfully at the monitors. They were flashing up numbers and bleeping occasionally, signalling trouble, and for an instant she was uncertain what to do.

'The duty nurse will keep an eye on her. We've done all we can for her for the moment.' He signalled to a nurse who was writing up names and treatments on the white board and she nodded and came over to them.

She was young, conscientious and good at her job, but she coloured prettily as James handed her the medication chart. 'I've given her the first dose of cardiac medication,' he said, 'so her heart rhythm should begin to settle before too long. Let me know if there are any adverse changes, will you?'

'I will.' The nurse smiled at him, and Sarah wondered at the softening of her features, the molten glow of her eyes and the pink curve of her mouth. It was odd how he had that kind of effect on the women all around him. She'd seen it before, with the female foundation-year doctors, as well as with the ancillary staff. They all fell for him.

Perhaps it was understandable. She was far from immune herself, but of necessity she'd learned to steel herself against his inherent charm. Like she'd said, self-preservation was a powerful instinct. She'd heard on the grapevine that he'd dated a couple of young women doctors, but rumour had it he didn't want to commit and he'd let the relationships slide when it looked as though they were getting too heavily involved.

They bought coffees from the cafeteria and took them outside to the landscaped grounds beyond the building. Here the earth was gently undulating, grassed over, with trees and shrubs providing a pleasing backdrop, and here and there were bench tables and seats where the hospital staff could sit and eat while enjoying the sunshine.

James led the way to a table that sat in the shade of a rowan tree. The tree's pinnate leaves were dark green, rustling softly in the light breeze, a pleasing contrast to the clusters of creamy white flowers that adorned its branches.

'I'm sorry you were upset just now,' he said. His eyes darkened. 'I could see that it was difficult for you, going back over what happened.'

She gave a brief, awkward smile. 'It's all right,' she said, in a voice that was suddenly husky with emotion. 'I was young and troubled, but I found a way of getting through it eventually…with Murray's help. He helped me to see things in a different light.'

'Murray. Your neighbour.' He said it in a measured tone, a muscle flicking in his jaw. 'He seems to have been a strong influence on your life…both then and now.'

'Yes. He persuaded me to take up medicine.' Truth to tell, James had actually been the biggest influence in her life, but she wasn't about to admit that to him.

He'd been patient, talking to her, making an effort to understand her, and she'd thrown it all back at him, too impulsive and reckless to care that he'd been trying to help her.

Her shoulders lifted in a negligent shrug. 'We kept in touch. Murray was always a good friend. He never judged me. Somehow he was just always there for me.'

'I suppose your father wasn't much help.'

'No, not much.' She pulled a face. 'I didn't get it at the time, why he didn't talk to me about my mother. He just clammed up, withdrew into himself. So, after I'd finished blaming myself for her leaving, I started to think it must have been his fault. He was the reason she'd walked away from us. He didn't talk about it. He kept his emotions locked up inside himself and I couldn't reach him so I started to kick out at anything and everything. I didn't care much about anything. And after the hurt there was just anger, a blinding, seething anger that seemed to grow and grow. The adults in my life had let me down and why should I worry any more about what anyone thought?'

'Do you ever hear from her or find out where she went?'

She shook her head and then sipped slowly at her coffee. 'Occasionally there would be cards. I think my dad tried to find her once, but by the time he tracked her down, she'd moved on. I know he wrote to her at the address he'd found, and a couple of months later there was a birthday card for me in the post. I was sixteen. It broke my heart.'

She rested her palm on the table, and he gently stroked the back of her hand as though he would comfort her in some small way. 'Did you ever try to get in touch with her?'

'Yes, I did, from time to time…when I got over my anger and frustration. I just wanted to know why she did it, why she went away without a word of warning. I wanted to understand how she could have been so heartless. So I wrote to the address my father had found and hoped that my letter would be forwarded on to her. I thought, if she could send cards, there must be a tiny bit of remorse for what she did, somewhere deep down. But she never replied.'

She pressed her lips together, making her mouth into a flat line. 'I still want answers, even now, but I haven't been able to find her. The Salvation Army made some enquiries for me, but nothing came of it. It's very frustrating.'

'Perhaps it would be better if you gave up on searching for her. It isn't getting you anywhere, is it?'

'I don't think I can do that. It eats away at me, the not knowing. I need answers, and somehow, without them, I don't feel as though I can move on.'

He shook his head. 'After all this time you have to find a way of putting it behind you. Going on the way you are, you might simply be raking up more heartache for yourself.'

Her chin lifted. 'Then that's the way it will have to be. I can't give up.'

They finished their coffee and went back to A and E. Sarah sought out the friends who had come along with Rachel to the emergency department and spent some time with them, trying to find out more about the demons that had driven this troubled young girl to drink herself into a coma. It seemed to her that it was a very thin thread that separated her from this teenager. By all accounts, both of them had to face up to insurmountable problems...or maybe the difficulty was that they weren't facing up to them.

At the end of her shift she was glad to go home and leave the worries of A and E behind her for a while. More patients had been admitted to the observation ward, and when she left the hospital Rachel was still unresponsive for the most part. It would be several hours before her blood alcohol level reached a safe point, and likewise the problems that the Ecstasy had caused with high blood pressure and overheating would take some time to resolve.

Murray had collected the children from school for her, and she spent half an hour chatting to him before going back to her own house with Sam and Rosie.

'My boss is coming to help out with getting the house shipshape,' she told the children as they had dinner together later in the warm kitchen. 'I'll be painting the walls in your room, Sam, so maybe you can play in the living room this evening. I don't want you and Rosie arguing while we're busy.'

Sam didn't answer, but his upper lip jutted out in a scowl, and it seemed to Sarah that might be a bad sign. He was obviously keeping his options open as far as keeping the peace was concerned.

'He had a fight with a boy called Ricky at school,' Rosie confided. 'Ricky ended up with a bruise on his leg and he told the teacher Sam did it.'

'You didn't have to tell,' Sam complained, his expression dark and his eyes giving out flint-like sparks.

'Yes, but Murray has the letter from the teacher,' Rosie said with a holier-than-thou attitude. She looked at Sarah. 'He must have forgotten to give it to you.'

There was a tap on the kitchen door at that moment, and Murray poked his head into the room. 'Is it all right if I come in?' he asked, and Sarah nodded.

'We were just talking about you,' she told him. 'Apparently you have a letter for me?'

He nodded, and held out an envelope. 'Sorry, it went out of my head when we were talking about your internet article. I came to give it to you as soon as I remembered.' He saw Sam's belligerent expression and added, 'Cheer up, old son. It could have been worse, and neither of you came out of it unscathed. Have you shown Sarah your war wounds?'

Sarah's jaw dropped. 'War wounds? What on earth happened?'

Sam began to fidget, hunching his shoulders as if he'd rather be elsewhere.

'Show me,' Sarah demanded, and he reluctantly held out his arm and rolled back the sleeve of his shirt. There were several red scratches along his forearm.

'I think you'd better explain,' she said, keeping a level tone.

'It wasn't nothin',' he muttered. 'Ricky said I couldn't play football 'cos I didn't have no football boots and I said I didn't need any, and I could play better football than him any day. Then we got into a fight.'

His grammar had gone to pieces, a sure sign that he was uptight. Sarah scanned the letter from the teacher. 'They're not taking any action because it happened outside the school grounds,' she said, and then added,

'Heavens, this all took place yesterday morning, after I dropped you off at school.' She looked at Murray, her eyes widening.

'The other parent complained to the head,' he explained. 'I didn't hear anything about it until the teacher handed me the letter today. Both boys have been reprimanded.'

'Hmm.' She glanced at Sam. 'Next time anything like this happens, you tell me straight away so that I know what I'm dealing with.' She sighed. 'And I suppose we'll have to get you some football boots. They weren't on the list, so how was I to know? We'd better go into town after I finish work tomorrow.'

Sam allowed himself an exultant grin. 'Yay!'

'Never mind "Yay",' she said. 'No more fighting.' The doorbell rang, and she stood up. 'That'll be James,' she murmured. 'Excuse me. I'll go and let him in.'

James was waiting patiently outside the front door. He looked incredibly sexy. He was dressed in casual clothes, black chinos teamed with a dark shirt that skimmed his flat stomach and draped smoothly over broad shoulders. He was long and lean and as she looked at him her heart missed a beat. Heat began to pool in her abdomen and an unbidden yearning clutched at her, causing the breath to catch in her lungs.

He studied her, those grey eyes all-seeing, assessing her in return, and a faint smile hovered on his lips. 'Aren't you going to invite me in?'

'Oh. Yes, of course. Come in.' She opened the door wider, stepping back a pace and waving him into the hallway. 'We're in the kitchen. We were just having a bit of a discussion about problems at school.'

He looked at her curiously. 'What sort of problems?'

'Boys. Fighting,' she muttered, as though that said it all.

'Uh-huh.'

They went into the kitchen, and she introduced him to Murray first of all. 'We met years ago at the rock-climbing club at the coast,' she said. 'Murray showed me all the things I needed to know, like how to use a belay device and hammer pitons into rock crevices for anchor points.' She frowned, seeing that the men were looking at one another with oddly quizzical expressions. 'Do you two actually know each other?'

'I think we may have met before,' James said, eyeing up Murray's lanky, relaxed figure. 'Didn't your company supply the equipment for one of the activity weekends on my father's estate? We held a gymkhana and a dog trial course, if I remember correctly. You came to help set everything up for the event.'

'That's right.' Murray was impressed. 'You've a good memory—that was some years ago.'

'Mmm.' James studied Murray, his grey eyes taking in everything about him, from his jeans and supple leather jacket to the square cut of his jaw and the protective, intent expression that came into his blue eyes when he glanced at Sarah.

Sarah thought back to those summer days she'd spent on the Benson estate. She remembered being invited to the events that were held there from time to time, and the gymkhana stood out particularly in her mind. She'd ridden one of the horses that day. Over the previous months James's father had had his stable manager teach her how to ride—maybe he'd taken pity on the girl whose mother had abandoned her. Whatever, she had been performing that day, and when she'd come to the end of a faultless round, she'd slid down from her horse into James's waiting arms. He'd laughed as he'd caught her, and in that moment, as his arms had closed about her, she had fallen hopelessly, instantly in love.

What girl wouldn't have lost her heart to a man as sexy and charismatic as James Benson? To a naïve six-teen-year-old, he was everything she'd ever dreamed about, and when he'd wrapped his strong arms around her she'd been in heaven, a state of bliss that she'd wanted to go on for ever and ever. She'd felt the warmth of him, his long, firmly muscled body next to hers, and as he'd steadied her and led her away to the refresh-ments tent, she'd felt that at last the world had granted her deepest heartfelt wish. He'd noticed her, he'd held her, and life couldn't get much better.

Except of course, it hadn't really been like that, had it? For James's part, he had simply been acting the host for his father's community endeavour, and it had been his role to make the contestants feel comfortable and at their ease. His natural charm had taken care of the rest.

She drew in a deep breath and tried to unscramble her brain. 'James is going to help with the renovation work,' she said now, breaking into the silence that had fallen between the two men.

'Ah, that's good. I'm glad you're getting some help.' Murray straightened, and perhaps he felt uncomfortable under James's dark scrutiny because he started towards the door. 'I'll leave you to it, then.' He glanced at the letter lying on the kitchen table. 'I wouldn't worry too much about that, if I were you.'

'No. Well, Sam is going to have to stop fighting and find some other way to solve his disputes.' She glanced at Sam, who responded with a look of benign innocence on his face.

Murray left and Sarah offered James coffee. 'We'll take it upstairs with us,' she suggested. 'I thought I'd make a start with the red paint in Sam's room.' She turned to the children. 'It means you'll have to share Rosie's room tonight,' she told Sam. 'Murray helped me to shift your bed in there earlier today,' she added.

Rosie's mouth opened in protest. 'Share with him? No way!' She placed her hands on her hips, taking a mutinous pose, and Sarah's mouth made a downward quirk.

'It's only for a couple of nights, so that the smell of paint can evaporate,' she said. 'Why don't you both go and call for the children next door? See if they want to play in the garden for a while, and after that you can go into the living room.'

Sam headed for the back door, quickly followed by Rosie, who was marshalling more arguments against sharing with her brother. 'You'd better keep your hands off my game pad,' she warned him, 'or you'll be sleeping on the landing.'

'See if I care.' The door swung shut behind them.

'They love each other really,' Sarah said. She frowned. 'At least, I think they do.'

James laughed. 'I guess we should get started on the room while we have the chance.'

'True. Who knows when things might erupt?'

All was peaceful, though, for the next hour or so, and Sarah found that she was beginning to relax in James's company. He worked on all three fireplaces, scrubbing hard to remove any rust and debris that had accumulated over the years, and then he cleaned everything down with a sponge and cloth.

'There shouldn't be any dust in the air to affect your paintwork,' he said as he worked with her in Sam's room. 'You're doing the far wall, so that's well away from here.'

They worked together in harmony, with music playing on the radio in the background, and every now and again they stopped to comment on a favourite tune or a particular melody.

'I danced to that music at Sam's christening,' Sarah commented some time later.

'It's a popular number even now.' He headed for the door. 'I'll go and wash my hands.'

She'd finished painting the wall by now, had tidied away brushes and roller, and was standing back to look at the result. It didn't look bad at all, and she'd actually managed to keep the paint off her hands and clothes. She rubbed moisturiser into her hands and turned around to study the fireplace.

James had applied a coat of red oxide to the heavy iron. At the weekend, he'd said, he would finish it off with the grate polish.

He came back from washing his hands in the bathroom to find her with a dreamy expression on her face. 'Sounds as though this tune has some special meaning for you,' he said, listening to the gentle rhythm of the music.

'I remember floating around the room feeling as though I was on a cloud.' She laughed. 'That was probably down to the wine that I had with the celebratory meal after the church service. And little Sam was so sweet, with his mop of black hair and his lovely blue-grey eyes that seemed to look deep into your soul. He was nine months old then, looking around and taking notice of everything, and I thought he was adorable… my half-brother, my family. I felt this huge surge of love for him.'

She closed her eyes, thinking about that moment, letting the music flow through her, over her and around her. 'The music stopped, and I looked at my stepmother. She was holding Sam in her arms and he was almost asleep. He had that soft, sleepy look that babies have, he was trying to stay awake and enjoy the fun, but his eyelids kept slowly closing, and Tracy was looking down at him with such love, such overwhelming happiness. And I…' She broke off, the words catching in her throat. 'I thought, Why couldn't my mother love me like that?'

James slid his arms around her. 'Don't do this to yourself, Sarah. You don't know why she left, what went through her mind. You have to find a way to move on.'

'I know…but I don't know how…'

He held her close, his hand gently stroking the length of her spine, drawing her near to him so that their bodies meshed and her soft, feminine curves melted against the hard contours of his strong, masculine frame.

'You said it yourself, everything has happened so quickly of late. You lost your father and Tracy and you found yourself responsible for two young children. Then there was the move here, the new job. It's no wonder that you're feeling this way—your emotions are all over the place because now that you finally have time to breathe and take it all in, it's all coming home to you. You haven't had time to grieve properly.'

'I suppose you're right. It hadn't occurred to me.' She leaned against him, accepting the comfort he offered, drinking in the warmth of his body, taking refuge in the arms that circled her, keeping her close.

He kissed her lightly on the forehead, a kiss as soft as gossamer. She could barely feel it, and yet his touch seared her, its aftermath racing through her body like flame. 'I'm right,' he murmured, his voice deep and soothing, smoothing a path along her fractured nerves. 'All this will pass, and you'll get your life back together, you'll see. You've done so well to come this far.'

She wanted him to kiss her again, to hold her and kiss her on the lips, her throat, along the creamy expanse of her shoulders. He could make everything all right again. He was the only one who could do it. She laid her palm lightly against his chest. Her whole body trembled with longing, even as she knew it couldn't happen.

She'd been here before, yearning for his kisses, wanting him, only the memory of that time still haunted her dreams. She'd been seventeen, and she'd learned that the family was to move to Devon to start a new life. A new life away from James. That was how she'd thought of it, and she'd dreaded going away and leaving him behind. He had been all she'd had in the world. Her father and Tracy had been wrapped up in one another and she had simply been an outsider, looking in. How was she going to let him know how much she wanted him?

Just a few drinks, that's all it had taken, an opened bottle of wine in the fridge...no one would notice that she'd helped herself. Her father would think Tracy had drunk it, and Tracy would imagine her husband had finished it off.

It was pure Dutch courage. It was what she'd needed to give her the confidence to go and find James and show him that he needed her as much as she needed him.

And the clothes, of course…they were important, they had to be just right, extra-special. She had to look her best. And that was where her bridesmaid's dress came in, the one she'd worn to her father's wedding. It was the perfect creation for her, an off-the-shoulder cream dress in a filmy, soft material that clung to her curves and draped itself gently around her ankles. How could he resist her? Surely he would want her, and he would show her once and for all that she was the only woman in the world for him?

All she had to do was go to him, find him in his apartment in the big country house. It was late autumn and he was home for Christmas, celebrating the beginning of his second year as a foundation doctor. She set off along the quiet, country lane to walk the half-mile to the estate.

James always left the side door unlocked until late at night, so it was easy to gain entrance to the north wing of the house. He was so startled, his eyes widening as she walked—no, sashayed—into his sitting room. Heady from the wine she'd drunk, she'd put her arms around him, letting her fingers trail through the silken hair at his nape, and she pressed her body close to his, her breasts softening against his chest. She lifted her face for his kiss. He had to want her. She wanted him, needed him desperately...

But there it all went wrong. His hands went around her in an involuntary motion, smoothing along the length of her spine, his palm coming to rest lightly on the curve of her hip. Then he sucked in his breath and his fingers gently circled her wrists, drawing her arms down from his neck, away from him.

She was stunned. This wasn't what she expected. This shouldn't be happening.

'I'm sorry, Sarah,' he said. 'I can't do this. You should go home. Come on, let me see you back to the house.' And he took off his jacket and wrapped it around her, taking her out of the room, out into the darkness of the night. The moon silvered the path, lighting their way, and she felt sick at heart. He didn't want her. He had rejected her, and she had made an almighty fool of herself. How could she face him ever again?

'Are you all right, Sarah?' The softly spoken words took her by surprise, and it was a moment before she realised that she was back in the present day, and they were standing in Sam's room, with the smell of paint filling the air and the music on the radio winding down to a soft murmur.

'I... Yes, I'm fine.' She eased herself away from him, her fingertips trailing across his shirtfront as she stepped back, putting distance between them. 'You're right,' she said huskily, 'these last few months have been an emotional roller-coaster. I'm probably overwrought and not thinking as clearly as I might.'

'Maybe you need to spend some time relaxing, in-stead of working on the house,' he suggested. 'A day on the beach, perhaps, or a visit to the village spring fayre. The change might do you a world of good.'

She nodded. 'I'm sure you're right. I'll have to sort something out.'

He smiled, looking at her a little oddly, as though he was trying to fathom what was going on in her head.

But she was safe enough, wasn't she? He couldn't possibly know what she'd been thinking, how close those memories had encroached on the here and now. Could he?

CHAPTER FOUR

'WILL you be coming along to the village's spring fayre?' James was writing up his patient's notes on the computer, but he looked up as Sarah came over to the desk.

'Um, when is it?'

He laughed. 'You're telling me you haven't seen all the notices posted up around the village?'

'I'm afraid I haven't.' She had the grace to look shamefaced. 'When I'm home I tend to dash about here and there, and the only things that tend to filter through to me are what to make for dinner, how did the laundry bin get full so quickly, and if Sam's managing to stay out of trouble.'

His mouth made a crooked line. 'Like I said, you need a break.'

'Yeah. Don't we all?' She bent her head so that he wouldn't see her reaction to his comment. That's what he'd told her last night, that she needed a break, and a wave of heat ran through her as she thought about it. She didn't want to recall those tender moments when she had been wrapped in his arms, but despite her misgivings the memory of that embrace had haunted her ever since. It had brought with it so many searing emotions, recollections of that earlier time when he had held her close. It was difficult enough seeing him every day, working with him, without being reminded of the foolish crush she'd had on him for all those long years.

To hide her discomfort, she began searching through the lab reports in the wire tray. 'So tell me about the fayre. I suppose I ought to support it if it's to do with the village.'

'It's tomorrow, from ten in the morning. Any money that's collected will go towards the fund for the new swimming pool—we want to build it in the grounds of the village school, so that all the local children will get the chance to learn how to swim from an early age. Being surrounded by the sea, as we are, it's really important that we keep them safe, but at the moment they have to go into the nearest town if they want to learn, and that's quite a drive for most villagers.'

She nodded. 'I see your point. It sounds like a really good cause. How's the fund doing?'

He smiled. 'Pretty well. I'm pleased with how things are going. We're almost there, and if the spring fayre brings in a goodly amount we should soon be able to start work on the pool.' He sat back in his chair, watching her, completely relaxed, his long legs stretched out in front of him. How could he be so laid back when she was distracted simply from being near him?

He was waiting for her answer and when she stayed silent he said, 'So, what do you say? Are you up for it?'

'Uh…yes, okay. I expect Rosie and Sam will enjoy a day out.'

'Good.' His mouth curved with satisfaction. 'I'll

come and collect you, if you like, at—what time? Would around midday suit you?'

'Um, thanks, that will be absolutely fine.' He was only offering to do that so that he could show her the way, wasn't he? He didn't have any deep-seated interest in her, other than as a colleague, so there was nothing for her to read into his suggestion, was there? He was good with everyone at work, helping them out whenever they had problems. Why would she be any different? A peculiar frisson of dismay crept through her at the thought, but she hastily pushed it away.

Anyway, wasn't one rejection enough for her? Why would she even entertain the idea of getting involved with him outside work? It didn't count that he was helping her with the house—he'd probably taken one look at it and made up his mind that she needed all the help she could get.

'Ought I to contribute something to the stalls?' She pursed her lips, trying to decide what she might take along. 'Some groceries, perhaps, or a cake? I could make a fruit cake and ice it. Rosie's really keen on baking these days and Sam's always up for joining in.'

He seemed to be quite taken with that suggestion. 'A cake sounds like a good idea,' he said cheerfully. 'We could have a guess the weight of the cake competition.'

She nodded, giving it some thought. 'That would certainly bring in some more money. It means I'll have to make a cake that looks fairly scrumptious if it's going to end up as a prize.' A niggling doubt crept in and she added in a rueful tone, 'Perhaps I should have had a bit more practice at cake decoration.' Then a thought struck her and her eyes narrowed on him. 'You're giving this whole thing the big sell—are you on the organising committee or something?'

'Uh...you could say that. The fayre's being held in the grounds of my house, and I've had quite a say in what's being included. And of course we have to make provision for all kinds of weather, so part of the house will be opened up as well.'

'Oh, I see.' She frowned. How would he come by the land that would be needed for such an enterprise? 'Going on past experience, an event like that could take up a big area...but you told me you weren't living on the family estate any more, didn't you? So how is it possible for you to do it?'

'You're right. I moved out some time ago. But I inherited a property from my great-grandparents—well, strictly speaking, my brother and I both shared the inheritance, but I bought out his half. He was happy for me to do that.'

'Even though he has a wife and children? Wouldn't he have welcomed the chance to have a property of his own instead of sharing with your parents?'

'Jonathan's comfortable staying on the family estate. There's plenty of room for them all there, and they have a separate wing to themselves. He acts as manager of the estate for my parents, so it's really convenient for him to be living on site.'

'I imagine it would be.' She hadn't reckoned on this, and it took some getting used to, discovering that James had not moved to an ordinary detached property, as she'd imagined, but instead he'd inherited another grand house. It just went to show that there was still this huge divide between them and perhaps she ought to have realised that his wealthy background would always be a part of him.

Giving herself a moment to absorb all this, she glanced at the paper in her hand and then frowned as she read through Nicola Carter's test results.

'Is something wrong?'

'Not wrong...a bit worrying, perhaps. I have the results here for Mrs Carter, the patient who collapsed after the road accident with bruising to the liver. From the looks of these lab-test results, she has a secondary adrenal insufficiency. Both the ACTH and the cortisol levels are low.'

His expression was thoughtful. 'We'd better do an MRI scan to see if anything's going on with the pituitary gland. In the meantime, we'll go ahead with steroid treatment and see how she responds to that.'

'I'll see to it. I'm going to look in on Rachel, too, to see how she's doing. Hopefully, she's over the worst as far as the drug abuse goes, and the alcohol should be out of her system by now, so I might be able to talk to her, and maybe find out if she needs counselling of some sort.'

'They all need counselling when they get into that state,' he said in a dry tone. 'It wasn't an unusual situation for her, by all accounts. Her blood-alcohol level was sky high, and drug-taking has been a common thing for her.'

'Well, I'll do what I can for her in the meantime. Are we going to move her on to a medical ward?'

'Yes, and Mrs Carter, too, as soon as we have the results of the scan.'

Sarah nodded, and hurried away to set things in motion. She was relieved to be able to put some distance between James and herself. It was more difficult for her than she had expected, working with him. It had shocked her to the core to relive all those old humiliating feelings last night, when she'd been in his arms. What must he think of her? And yet he'd said nothing, either then or now…and he'd certainly never commented on her immature, futile attempt at seduction when she was in her teens. It was hard to know whether that made things better or worse.

The rest of the day passed quickly, with a flurry of emergencies being brought into A and E after a traffic accident and a near-drowning off the coast at Land's End. They brought their patient, an eleven-year-old boy, back from the brink of death, and Sarah couldn't help thinking that James was right about the need for swimming lessons. The sea could be a dangerous place for the unwary.

Rachel was able to sit up in bed by now, and the endotracheal tube had been removed so that she was breathing unaided, but she looked pale and unhappy when Sarah went to see her. Her long brown hair was lank and her hazel eyes were dull and lacking in any kind of interest in her surroundings.

'Hello, Rachel,' Sarah greeted her. 'How are you feeling today?'

'Tired. My chest hurts… I'm a bit breathless.'

Sarah nodded, and checked the heart and respirations monitor. 'It's an after-effect of the Ecstasy you took,' she explained. 'You've had some problems with your heart rhythm, but things are beginning to settle down. That would have been worrying enough on its own, but the alcohol added even more complications. It does seem as though you've set yourself on a bit of a downward spiral. I'd like to think we could help you to get your life back on course. Maybe we could talk about anything that's bothering you.'

'There's no point.' The girl turned her head away.

'There's a lot of point, surely? Your friends have been to see you, I hear. They're obviously very worried about you.'

Rachel didn't react, apart from a slight movement of her shoulders, as though she could scarcely find the energy to respond. Sarah said softly, 'Is there anyone we can contact for you—your parents, for instance? I saw from your notes that you're living in a flat, so I presume you left the family home a while ago.'

Rachel shook her head. 'There's no one.'

'I'm sorry.' Sarah frowned. 'Do you want to tell me about it? Did something happen to your parents?'

'No. Not really. We were always arguing, it was a bad atmosphere, and I decided it would be better if I moved out. My brother left a couple of years ago, and I thought I'd do the same.'

'Do you keep in touch with your brother?'

'Not lately. I used to see Harry every now and again, but since I left home last year I haven't heard from him. He was sharing a house with a friend, but he's not there any more.'

'But you used to get on well together?'

Rachel nodded. She closed her eyes, and Sarah could see that even this short conversation had been too much for her. If they could find this brother, perhaps he could do something to lift his sister out of this self-destructive pattern of behaviour. 'I'll leave you to get some rest,' she said quietly. 'Try to drink plenty of fluids—I see your friends have left you some orange squash. The nurses will keep your water jug topped up. Just ask them if you need any help while you're not able to get out of bed.'

After work, Sarah picked up the children from Murray's house and took them into town to buy football boots for Sam and new shoes for Rosie. 'I think we'll pick up some ingredients for sugar paste and some food colouring, while we're about it,' she told them.

'Why? Are we making cakes?' Rosie asked. 'We did sugar paste at school and made all these little flowers. They were lovely. And you can eat them, too.'

'Well, just one cake,' Sarah explained, 'for the village fayre. We'll make it after we've had our evening meal. And then tomorrow, when it's completely cool, we'll have a go at icing it.' It meant she would be spending what was left of the evening searching the internet for tips on how to decorate cakes but, then, it was all in a good cause.

'There we are... I think that's turned out pretty well, don't you?' she said later that evening, as she took the rich fruit cake from the oven and slid it onto a rack.

'It looks yummy,' Rosie commented, admiring the luscious, deep golden brown cake.

'And it smells good,' Sam agreed. He pulled a face. 'But I think we ought to be able to keep it after the fayre and eat it.'

'Mmm. Sorry about that.' Sarah smiled. 'But whoever guesses the weight gets to win it and take it home.'

His expression brightened. 'We'll just weigh it, then,' he said, licking his lips in anticipation.

'Away with you! That would be cheating.' She laughed. 'Anyway, I'm sure there'll be lots more goodies for you to try when we go to the fayre tomorrow.'

The next day, Sarah was up early, anxious to ice the cake before James arrived to take them over to his house. She was a little bit apprehensive, thinking about the day ahead, being with James away from work, and the only way she could counter those feelings was to keep busy. She covered the cake with a layer of marzipan and then spread the white icing over the top and sides.

It had been a long, long while since she had spent a day out with James, and it was one thing to do that on neutral territory, but somehow the prospect of being with him on his home ground was a different thing altogether. It was far too intimate a setting, and not at all what she had envisaged when she'd made up her mind to keep things on a professional basis between them. She gave a rueful smile. Her plans in that regard had probably been scuppered from the outset, what with having lunch with him and with him helping her to renovate the house. Hadn't it always been that way in her dealings with James? Whatever she decided, life had a way of turning everything upside down.

'What are we going to do?' Rosie asked, yawning as she came into the kitchen some time later. She blinked, trying to accustom her eyes to the sunshine that filtered into the kitchen through the slats in the blinds at the window. 'Are we going to cover it with icing sugar flowers, or ribbons and bows? Or both?' She looked at the collection of decorative materials that Sarah had set out on the pine table.

'I'm not sure yet,' Sarah said. 'We'll have to think about it while we have breakfast.'

'I think we should do a water picture, if it's to get money for the pool,' Sam announced, coming to join them at the table. He was still dressed in his pyjamas, and his shoulders slumped as though he would much rather be snuggled up in bed but hadn't wanted to miss out on anything.

'That's actually quite a good idea,' Rosie said in a surprised tone. She looked at her brother as though she didn't quite know him. 'It'll be good to have a swimming pool at the school. Everyone will be able to have lessons, or practise, won't they?' Then she frowned. 'Mum taught us how to swim when we were small. It was fun, and we used to go to the pool every week. She said we were her little water nymphs.' Her grey eyes clouded momentarily and Sam's expression dissolved into sudden anguish.

Sarah sucked in a silent breath. 'Maybe we should make this a special cake, then,' she suggested, thinking quickly. 'We could do a design to show we're thinking of your mother, with a garden pond, perhaps, and two water nymphs sitting on flower petals nearby. What do you think?'

'Oh, yes, that'd be brilliant.' Sam was smiling now, and Rosie had a thoughtful look about her.

'We should have a blue colour for the pond,' she said, 'and there should be some water lilies on it. You'll need green sugar paste for those, and white and yellow for the flowers.' She inspected the bottles of food colouring that were set out on the table. 'And then some bigger flowers for the water nymphs to sit on.'

'Or they could be in trees, with little houses in them.' Sam was looking pleased with himself, excited about the project. 'And there could be a frog on the pond and a boy fishing.'

'That sounds lovely, but let's not get too carried away,' Sarah laughed. 'The simpler the better, I think. After all, we only have a few hours before James comes to pick us up, and I'm not exactly used to doing this sort of thing.'

By the time James arrived at midday, they were just about ready, with the children dressed and raring to go and Sarah putting the finishing touches to her make-up. She was wearing dark blue jeans and a smooth-fitting cotton top, and she'd pinned her hair up into a loose topknot.

'Hi. Are you all set?' James asked. He gave her an admiring glance and then relieved her of the holdall she was carrying and tested the weight with his hand. 'Heavens, what have you packed in here? We're going for an afternoon out, not a week's trekking expedition.' He grinned.

'It's just a few extras—an emergency first-aid kit and clothes in case the weather turns to rain, or one or other of the children manages to fall into a mud pile or some such.'

He laughed. 'That's hardly likely to happen, is it?'

She sent Sam a surreptitious look. 'Don't you believe it,' she whispered. 'I still haven't recovered from taking them to the zoo last month.'

'That wasn't my fault,' Sam put in with a frown. There was obviously nothing wrong with his hearing.

'I didn't start it. I was looking at the monkeys and Rosie got fed up waiting and pushed me out of the way.'

'Did not!' Rosie let out a shriek of indignation. 'I was trying to get by him.'

'Did too. And so I pushed her back and then we got into a fight and we both ended up rolling down the slope. Wasn't my fault it had been raining and the ground was all messy.'

Sarah groaned. 'Oh, please…don't remind me.'

James looked puzzled. 'I take it things got a bit out of hand?'

She nodded. 'As they do quite often.' She studied him briefly. 'You seem surprised. But you must know how these things are…you're used to children, aren't you? You said your brother had a boy and a girl.'

'Yes, but they're only one and two years old.' He gave her a doubtful look. 'There are never any problems with them…not that I can see, anyway.'

'Oh, dear.' She gave him a sympathetic look. 'I can see this is all new to you. For myself, I've watched Rosie and Sam growing up, and I have friends whose offspring are always up to something or other, so nothing much surprises me any more where children are concerned. You've been well and truly sheltered, haven't you, living the bachelor lifestyle these last few years?'

'I suppose I have.' He smiled as they walked out to his car, a sporty, silver streak of mouth-watering beauty. It had a soft top, and the hood was down to leave the occupants free to enjoy the sunshine and fresh breeze. 'Hop in the back, you two,' he said to the children, tossing the holdall into the boot. He glanced at Sarah. 'Is that the cake you're carrying? Do you want me to put it in here along with the holdall?'

'I think I'd rather keep it with me,' she said, guarding the cake tin as though it was something precious, not to be let out of her sight. 'After all the work we've put into it, I want to be sure we get it there in one piece.'

'I can't wait to see it. Do I get to have a peek now?'

'Okay.' She carefully prised the lid off the tin. 'You won't be able to see the sides this way. Rosie and Sam decided we needed pale green fronds all the way round, to represent reeds.'

He looked into the tin and gave a low whistle of appreciation.

'So, you like it?' she asked.

'I certainly do. That's a real work of art. If I won it, I wouldn't be able to bring myself to cut into it.' He glanced at her, his gaze full of admiration. 'What a brilliant idea, to have a water theme. I love those little water nymphs.'

She nodded. 'That came from Sam. He's quite a deep thinker, underneath it all. And both of the children helped, especially with the flowers and leaves.' She'd made the wings for the water nymphs herself, lovely gossamer creations made from golden spun sugar strands.

'I can see why you want to keep it safe,' he said, waiting as she carefully replaced the lid on the tin. He held open the car door for her as she slid into the passenger seat. 'You're amazing...definitely a woman of hidden talents.'

She mumbled something incoherent in return and he gave her a quizzical look as he slid behind the wheel of the car. As if he'd ever wanted to explore those talents. The thought came to her unbidden, and she swiftly pushed it away. She had to keep her mind off that track. The past was done with, finished, and it was high time she acknowledged that, if only for her own peace of mind.

He followed the coast road for a while, and then turned off down a winding country lane. At first there were houses clustered together but these gradually became more and more isolated until finally they came to what must have been a large farmhouse at one time. James took them along a wide driveway, bordered on either side by manicured lawns, where stalls were set out. Some displayed goods for sale, while others offered games to be played and prizes to be won.

'Here we are,' he said, pulling up in front of the house and cutting the engine. 'This is my place.'

'Wow.' Sam was impressed. He jumped out of the car and stared up at the wide frontage of the two-storey building. 'Do you live here all by yourself?'

'I do. But a lady comes from the village to clean up for me a couple of days a week. She does a bit of cooking, too, because she's afraid I might starve to death, left to my own devices.'

Rosie frowned. 'Would you really? Starve, I mean?' She was obviously worried by that. 'You could always put stuff in the microwave, you know. It's easy to do that. That's what my mum used to do when we all wanted different things.'

'That's what I do, too, sometimes.' He smiled at her. 'You should come and see my kitchen. I've just had it remodelled, and there's a microwave and a tabletop slow-cooker in there, as well as a built-in oven—all kinds of equipment that I still have to learn to use.'

'You should ask Sarah to help you out,' Rosie suggested helpfully. 'She's had to learn how to do all sorts of cooking 'cos she says we're not allowed to eat rubbish. We have to grow and be strong and healthy.'

Sam flexed his muscles. 'I've been eating lots,' he said. 'I'm going to get big so's I can beat Ricky Morton.' He began to jab at the air with his fists, like a boxer.

Sarah raised her eyes heavenwards. 'What did I say about no fighting?' she reminded him.

'Yeah, well…if he comes at me, I'll be ready for him.' He made another lunge with his arm.

Sarah looked once more at the house as they started to walk towards the stalls. It was built of mellow, sand-coloured stone, and there were lots of Georgian-style windows, with an entrance porch at the mid-point. Jasmine rambled around and over the porch canopy, its waxy, star-shaped white flowers adding a purity and delicate beauty to the archway. The walls were covered in part with dark green ivy, lending the house an old-world charm. 'It's lovely,' she said, smiling appreciatively.

'I'm glad you like it.' James looked fondly at his home, set against a backdrop of mature trees and colourful shrubs. 'It's always had a special place in my heart—not just because of the house, though it is beautiful, but because my grandparents lived here before they bought the house where my parents live now. There are so many memories locked up in this place that I couldn't bear to see the house go onto the open market. It belongs within the family.'

There was a far-away look in his eyes. 'My brother and I used to come here on visits, and we had our own rooms when we stayed over.' He winced. 'After my grandparents left, it was let out as apartments for holidaymakers for a number of years. It's taken a while but it's good to have it restored to a family home once more.'

She nodded, understanding how he must feel. 'And to think I worry about my small renovations,' she said with a laugh. 'I couldn't even begin to tackle something like this.'

'Can we go on the bouncy castle?' Rosie asked, looking eagerly towards where children were jumping and squealing with delight. 'I can see Frances from school, and her brother, Tom. He's in Sam's class.'

'Yes, that's okay. We'll be looking at the stalls over here when you've finished.'

The children hurried away. 'We could put your cake on the table next to where the raffle is being drawn,' James suggested. 'One of the helpers made up a "Guess the weight" chart, so there's nothing else that needs to be done.'

'All right.' They put the cake in pride of place on the table, and straight away a small crowd formed, oohing and aahing over it.

'It's already looking as though that will be a money-spinner,' James said. 'Perhaps Rosie was right...you could give me a few tips on how to cook.' He slid an arm around her waist as they walked away, drawing her close to him and setting up a tingling response in her that rippled through her from head to toe.

'I'd be happy to do that, though I can't see you spending much time in the kitchen, state-of-the-art equipment or not,' she answered, trying to ignore the heat that was spreading through her. 'You're far more likely to drop by Martha's shop for doughnuts and sticky buns.' She looked him over, lean and muscled in chinos and T-shirt, with not an ounce of fat to spare. 'Heaven knows how you manage to stay so fit looking.'

He grinned. 'It must be all that hands-on exercise I get in A and E that does it. It certainly seems to work for you, anyway.' His glance shimmered over her, and Sarah felt a small glow start up inside her. At least he wasn't calling her skinny any more.

'I don't think that's just down to the work at the hospital. There are two energetic youngsters who have a big hand in keeping me on my toes.'

'True.' They wandered around the stalls for a while, trying their hands at spinning the wheel to win a soft toy, and knocking down skittles for a bag of sweets. Rosie and Sam came to join them after a while, playing hoopla and firing water pistols at toy ducks to see if they could knock them off the stand. Then the children sat for a few minutes while their faces were painted and they were transformed into a glittery princess and a fiery tiger.

'You look fantastic,' Sarah told them, and James nodded in agreement.

'But we came here with Rosie and Sam,' he said with a puzzled frown. 'Any idea where they've gone?'

Rosie giggled.

They spent some time at the barbecue, munching on succulent chicken and rice, kebabs and salad. Then Rosie and Sam wandered over to one of the toy stalls, keen to spend some of their pocket money on new treasures. They came back a few minutes later, eager to grab Sarah's attention.

'Can we go round with Frances and Tom for a bit?'

'There are pony rides round the back of the house,' Sam added, 'and we want to have a go. Their mum says it's all right. She said we could meet up with you in the refreshments tent at four o'clock, if that's all right with you.' He pointed towards Frances's mother in the distance, who mouthed carefully and gesticulated that she would look after them.

Sarah nodded and mouthed 'Thank you' in return. She'd met and talked with Kate Johnson on several occasions and knew she would carefully watch over them. 'Okay. That's fine with me. If you need us before then, we'll be out here somewhere, looking at the stalls.'

'Or maybe we'll be in the house,' James put in. 'I thought I might show Sarah around.'

'Okay.' The children ran off to join their friends, and James took Sarah's arm, guiding her towards the tombola table. 'Let me buy you some tickets,' he said. 'I'm sure you'd love to win a basket of fruit, wouldn't you?'

'I certainly would,' she said, eyeing the basket that had pride of place amongst the beans, sauces and pickles. Instead, she ended up with a jar of strawberry jam. 'That's an excellent jam,' she said, looking closely at the jar. 'I love it, but Sam will pick out all the strawberries and put them to one side.'

'Tut-tut…' James smiled, his mouth crooking attractively. 'That's sacrilege.' They reached the coconut shy, and he took careful aim with a wooden ball, hitting the target full on.

A minute or so later he weighed the coconut in his hand and said in a droll tone, 'I don't even like coconut...and have you ever tried to open up one of these things?'

She chuckled. 'I dare say a hammer and chisel would come in pretty handy.' She walked with him to the plant stall, picking out a selection of plants for her small garden. 'I don't have a lot of room out back,' she told him, 'but I thought I could brighten the borders with begonias and marigolds. And I love antirrhinums, so I have to find a spot for those.' She gazed into the distance, looking at his beautifully landscaped gardens, where flowering shrubs added swathes of colour to the front of the house. There were low-spreading berberis with an abundance of orangey-yellow flowers, magnificent cotoneasters and attractive yellow cytisus.

'I'll carry these for you,' James said, helping to place her purchases in a plastic plant tray. He wedged the coconut in one corner. 'Perhaps we should drop these off at the house, and I'll give you the grand tour?'

'That sounds good to me.' She smiled at him, and realised that she had enjoyed these last few hours. Away from work, relieved of responsibilities for an hour or two, she'd been able to relax, and she discovered that being with him was fun. They talked, shared anecdotes, and took pleasure in the simple things of life. Perhaps she was living dangerously, being this close to him, watching him smile as he looked around and saw how everyone was making the most of their day out, but for the moment she was glad to cast her anxieties to one side.

'I've had quite some time to make the changes here,'

he said as he led the way into the house. Some of the rooms had been opened up to the visitors to the fayre, and French doors were open to allow easy access. There were cake stalls in here, and a table set up with a tea urn and cups and saucers. A few tables and chairs had been laid out so that people could take a few minutes to sit and chat over a cup of tea, with cake or scones, or even appetising sandwiches cut into small squares.

'Let's go through to the rooms that aren't being used for the fayre,' James suggested, taking her through an archway into a spacious hall. He'd taken the precaution of labelling the doors in here with signs saying 'Private'. They went into a large room, filled with light from a number of tall windows along one side. 'I use this as a study,' he said. 'If I need to keep up with the latest medical research, I come in here to sit at the desk and use the computer. Or if I want to read or listen to music, I have everything I need in here.'

'You certainly have a lot of books,' Sarah remarked, looking around. Bookshelves lined one wall, filled with an assortment of reading material, from medical and scientific volumes to travel books and a collection of the latest bestsellers. There was an armchair by the open fireplace, cosy and inviting, with well-stuffed cushions and a footstool close by. 'I could curl up in here for a week, just reading the murder mysteries you have on this shelf alone.' She trailed a finger over the spine of one novel, her eyes shining. 'I love anything by this writer,' she said. 'I've read everything he's ever published.'

'You're welcome to drop by any time and make yourself at home,' he offered, his grey glance moving over her like the lick of flame. 'I'd be more than happy to have you spend time here.'

Heat filled her cheeks. Was this how he managed to charm all the women at work? She was more than tempted to take him up on his offer, but a cautious inner voice warned her that it could only lead to trouble.

'Seriously, if you want to borrow any of the books, that's fine, just help yourself.' He smiled at her. 'I might have known you'd have a taste for the more exciting, edge-of-the-seat kind of writing. That daredevil, always-up-for-a-challenge girl has never really gone away, has she?'

'Oh, I wouldn't say that. I've learned that there are other kinds of challenge, like medicine, for example, that can be just as stimulating.'

'Yes, you're right.' He nodded, becoming serious once more. 'I think I've always wanted to be a doctor deep down, especially since I realised that you can make a difference by stepping in when someone's seriously ill or suffering from life-threatening trauma. I wanted to be first on the scene, with the ability to save lives—but you need to have a good team working with you. That's why I try to get the best of both worlds, by working in the hospital and outside with the air ambulance. It makes for a good balance, and stops the work from becoming mundane.'

'Yes, I'm with you there.'

They wandered from room to room, and it became clear that he had an eye for what was elegant and uncluttered. Everywhere was tastefully furnished, with colours that reflected nature, soft greens, pale gold and shades of russet. There were period pieces here and there—a couple of Hepplewhite chairs and a Georgian inlaid card table in the study, and a grandfather clock and oak settle in the sitting room.

The floorboards here were covered with luxurious oriental rugs and there was a wood-burning stove to provide warmth on chilly evenings.

The kitchen was just as he had said, completely fitted out with modern equipment, all discreetly blended with natural oak cupboards and marble worktops, and an island bar where you could sit and enjoy a cup of coffee while watching TV on a pull-down screen. At one end of the room there was a table and chairs next to the window that overlooked the landscaped garden. On another wall there was an antique oak dresser displaying beautiful hand-painted crockery.

'Mmm…you have everything you could possibly want in here,' she said. 'It's a dream kitchen. It would be a crime not to whip up some delicious meals in here.'

'I suppose so…though I've learned I can get by quite happily on take-away food, especially since the Chinese restaurant set up in the village a few months ago. They do a fantastic chop suey and egg fried rice.'

'Oh, don't!' she said on a soft sigh. 'I've eaten lunch, but I could still work my way through chop suey, chow mein and sweet and sour chicken. They're my absolute favourites.'

He chuckled. 'Perhaps we'd better move on from the kitchen. I'll show you upstairs.'

He led the way, showing her onto a wide landing, where several doors led off in various directions. 'There are four bedrooms, all with their own en suites,' he told her. They walked from one to the other, and Sarah was impressed by each one in turn.

'What do you think?' he asked. 'I've done them out in pale, restful colours, and carpeted them so that they're quiet and comfortable. I know some people don't like carpets, but I tend to wander about in bare feet first thing in the morning, and having wool underfoot seems to make life so much more relaxing.'

'I think they're just perfect. Especially this master bedroom.' She could imagine him padding about in here, bare-chested, yawning and stretching as he looked out of his window onto the garden below. This room was filled with his presence...everything in here reflected his calm, understated vitality. It was something she'd always admired in him, that effortless way he had of moving, all that latent energy waiting to be unleashed. And now...now she began to feel hot and bothered, overwhelmed by a sudden rush of hormonal feverishness. A pulse started to throb at the base of her throat and her chest felt tight.

'Are you all right?' He moved closer to her, searching her face, a small frown indenting his brow, and for once she couldn't hide the flush of heat that swept along her cheekbones. Small beads of perspiration broke out on her forehead.

'I'm fine. A bit hot, that's all,' she said huskily. 'Perhaps we should go.'

He shook his head. 'Sit down for a while. You look as though you're going to faint or something.' He waved a hand towards the bed. 'I'll open a window.'

'No, I'll be fine, really. There's no need for you to do

that. Perhaps the salad dressing I had earlier was a little salty. I should have had something to drink.'

'I'll get you some water. But you need to sit down,' he insisted, taking her gently by the arm and leading her over to the bed. 'In fact, maybe you should lie down for a while.' He felt her forehead with the back of his hand. 'You're really very hot.'

'I'm... It's nothing, really...' Her voice faded, and suddenly as James moved away from the bed it seemed like a good idea if she were to lie back for a while. Perhaps he was right after all. Maybe it wasn't hormones that were troubling her. She'd rushed about yesterday evening, seeing to the children, preparing the cake and studying cake decoration late into the night. And then from early this morning she'd been on the go, sorting the laundry, doing the chores and icing the masterpiece. And there'd been the notes she'd had to finish for her internet article. She'd been working to a deadline...

Her eyelids were heavy. It wouldn't hurt to close them for a second or two, would it? She heard him moving about in the bathroom, that gloriously cool room with the bathroom suite that gleamed palely and the ceramic tiled walls that reflected exquisite good taste. Her mouth was dry, and she could feel heat rising along the column of her throat. It felt damp to the touch.

There was something attached to her arm. She looked at it in vague disbelief. A blood-pressure monitor? James was taking her blood pressure?

'What are you doing?' she said, frowning, a headache starting at her temples.

'Your blood pressure's way too high,' James murmured, releasing the cuff from around her arm. 'No wonder you felt strange. Here, drink this.' He slid a hand behind her shoulders and gently raised her to a sitting position. With his other hand, he held a glass to her lips and she felt the cold drops of water trickle into her mouth.

She drank thirstily, and when she had finished he carefully laid her down again.

'You should get some rest,' he said, giving her a concerned look. 'I think you've probably been overdoing things lately. With that, and the move from Devon to Cornwall, and taking on the care of the children, you've had a lot to take on board. Your body's telling you to slow down, take time to breathe.'

She tried to sit up. 'The children,' she said. 'I should go and take over from Kate.'

'No. I'll see to it. You stay here. Try to get some sleep. There's nothing to bother you here, no one to worry about. I'll see to everything.'

'I'm so sorry,' she muttered. 'I can't believe this is happening. It has been such a lovely afternoon.'

'It still is,' he said, his mouth tilting at the corners. He laid a hand lightly on her shoulder, and she thought for a moment that he was going to brush her cheek with his hand, but then he brought his fingers down to her cotton top and he slowly began to undo the buttons at her throat.

'I... You...' She tried to protest, but the words wouldn't come out, and she simply stared at him, wide eyed, her lips parting a fraction.

'There's no need for you to panic,' he said. 'I'm not trying to take advantage of you. I'm only undoing the

first few buttons to cool you down. There's nothing for
you to worry about.'

'No?'

It was a query, and he answered with a smile. 'Any
other time, maybe it might have been different...but
right now I want to look after you,' he said. 'You'll
be safe here, I promise. Close your eyes and get some
sleep.'

Any other time... Her mind did a strange kind of
flip as she absorbed that, but then caution overtook her
once more. 'The children...' she said, her voice slurring
as weariness overcame her. 'You don't know how to...'

'They'll be fine. I'll let them loose on my DVD collection. And when they're tired of that, we'll make supper.'

'All right.' She closed her eyes and let herself sink
into the soft, cushioning duvet. 'Thanks.'

She didn't know what was happening to her but it
was sheer bliss to simply lie here and do nothing, to let
the healing power of sleep overtake her.

Her mind drifted, oblivion taking over. She thought
she felt him move closer, lean down and brush her forehead with a kiss that was as soft as a cotton-wool cloud.

But he wouldn't do that, of course. She must be
dreaming.

CHAPTER FIVE

SARAH slowly opened her eyes. She wasn't sure what had woken her, but the room was dark, and for a while she lay there, trying to recall where she was and what had happened. The last thing she remembered as she'd drifted away had been the heavenly feel of the mattress beneath her, as though she was being enveloped in softness. Later, she'd stirred, feeling a chill in the air, but soon afterwards there had been the sensation of something floaty being draped over her, and she'd sunk back into a blissful, deep sleep.

Now she tried to sit up, her eyes becoming accustomed to the shadows and the faint glow of moonlight that seeped into the room through the curtains.

'I didn't mean to disturb you,' James said softly, his voice deep and reassuringly calm. He switched on the bedside lamp, and a pool of golden light shimmered around her. 'I saw that you were a bit restless, so I made some hot chocolate.'

'Oh, thank you, that was thoughtful of you,' she murmured, still drowsy. She frowned. 'What time is it? How can it be dark? Surely I haven't slept for all that long?'

He placed a tray on the bedside table and sat down

on the edge of the wide bed. 'It's around ten o'clock. Once you settled down, you were well away.'

'Oh, no... I can hardly believe it. How could I have done that?' It suddenly struck her that she was supposed to be looking after the children, and she sat up straight in a panic. 'The children...'

'They're fine. They're fast asleep in the guest rooms. I told them they could sleep in their underwear for tonight.'

'But... Oh, this is awful. I let them down. I should go to them...'

He laid a hand on her shoulder and gently pressed her back against the pillows. 'You don't have to go anywhere. I explained to them that you were very, very tired and that you needed to rest. Of course, they wouldn't take my word for it and they insisted on coming up here to see you. Once they knew you hadn't been kidnapped or whisked away anywhere, they were fine. They watched a DVD and then we made sandwiches and popcorn.'

'You had popcorn in your kitchen?' She sent him a doubtful look and he grinned, handing her a mug of hot chocolate.

'Drink that. It'll help you settle for the night. The popcorn was Sam's. He bought a bag from the food stall and Rosie showed us how to heat it up in the microwave. I had no idea you could do that with corn.'

Her mouth curved. 'Well, I guess we learn something new every day.' She sipped the creamy chocolate and sighed with contentment. 'This is delicious.' Then she frowned. 'I really should get them home.'

'No, you don't have to do that.' He shook his head. 'It would be a shame to wake them.'

She chewed at her lower lip. 'We've been a lot of trouble to you, disturbing your peace. You probably had plans for this evening.'

'I didn't, beyond finishing off the fireplaces at your house.' He laughed. 'How sad is that?'

'Oh, enormously sad, for a man in his prime.' She laughed with him. 'Seriously, though, thanks for taking care of Sam and Rosie. It can't have been easy for you if you're not used to children.'

'It was okay.' A small line etched its way into his brow. 'They never stop, do they, kids? You think you have them settled, that everything's sorted, and they come up with something you never thought of…like "Can we sleep in a tent in the garden?" That was Sam. And "Why don't we make a spaghetti Bolognese?" That was Rosie. "You only need mince and tomato puree and herbs," she said, "and spaghetti, of course." Which would have been fine, seeing that I had some herbs in the kitchen.'

'And the rest of the ingredients?'

'Unfortunately, no.' He shook his head, his mouth making a wry shape. 'She doesn't have a very high opinion of my culinary efforts, I'm afraid.'

She smiled, swallowing more of the chocolate, before looking at him curiously. 'Did you ever think about having a family of your own? I mean, seeing your brother settled with his wife and children, did you think you might want to do that some time?'

'Some time, maybe, with the right woman.' His gaze rested on her intently for a moment or two, his gaze dark and unreadable, then he shrugged awkwardly and appeared to give the matter some thought. 'I've been too busy, up to now, with one thing and another, working my way up the career ladder. There have been a lot of specialist exams, different hospital jobs along the way. A wife and family probably wouldn't have fitted in too well with all that.'

'I suppose not.' Was that the reason he hadn't wanted to get more deeply involved with any of the women he had dated? From what she'd heard back at the hospital, there were more than a couple of women who mourned the fact that he hadn't wanted more than a light-hearted romance. She put down the mug.

His glance trailed over her, lingering on the burnished chestnut of her hair that framed the pale oval of her face, before he let it glide over the silken smoothness of her arms. 'What about you? I'd have expected someone to have snatched you up by now.'

She shifted a little under his dark-eyed scrutiny. She was still dressed in jeans and cotton top, but her buttons were undone, exposing the creamy swell of her breasts, and the light from the lamp added a soft sheen to her bare arms. She was covered with a light duvet, and now she pulled this up around her. 'I don't think I'm settling-down material, I'm afraid. I have this problem believing in happy ever after.'

'Ah…yes.' There was a regretful note in his voice. 'I can see how you might feel that way. When your mother went away, she left you with a scar that refuses to heal, didn't she?'

She glanced at him briefly from under her lashes. Her mother hadn't been the only one to do that to her, although the pain he'd caused her had been done unknowingly. 'Something like that.'

'But you've had boyfriends?' He was looking at her intently, a faint glitter in his eyes.

She nodded. 'Some.' She wasn't going to enlarge on that. Either they'd become too keen and she had ended the relationships, or they just hadn't gelled with her. Anyway, there was only one man she'd ever really wanted and he'd made it pretty clear years ago that he didn't want her.

James laid his hand over hers. 'You should get some sleep,' he said. 'It'll do you the world of good to rest and rid yourself of your cares for a while. I'll look in on the children, but I don't think you need have any worries on that score.'

'But this is your room... I'm in your bed.' She tried to sit upright once more but the duvet hindered her, wrapping itself around her.

'Mmm...' His mouth quirked wickedly and there was a gleam in his eyes as his gaze shimmered over her. 'I'd be more than happy to join you...breathtakingly happy, in fact...but I've a feeling that would be a big mistake. You're vulnerable right now, and you'd probably hate me in the morning.'

She drew in a sharp breath, her eyes widening. Was he really, actually saying that he wanted her? She made a second attempt to sit up.

He gently urged her back down, laying his hands on her shoulders in such a way that stirred up a fever inside her. 'Relax,' he said. 'I'll be in the room next door. If there's anything you need, just call out.'

The mere thought of doing that made her heart begin

to throb heavily in her chest, banging against her rib-cage. Should she wind her arms around him and tell him just how much she wanted to keep him close? What if she were to call out for him in the night and wait for him to come to her? Would he reject her this time, as he had done once before? Undoubtedly not, from the looks of things...but dared she risk everything in doing that?

But then he stood up, looking down at her for a moment or two before heading towards the door. She gave a soft sigh of relief mingled with regret. She wasn't thinking straight. How could she even imagine how it would be to lose herself in him...this man who couldn't commit?

After he'd gone, she switched off the lamp and lay down, snuggling under the warmth of the duvet. Her body ached with longing for what might have been.

In the morning, after a deep sleep, she woke feeling renewed, refreshed and full of energy. When she drew back the curtains, it was to a bright day with the sun making the colours of nature even more vivid than usual. She opened the bedroom window, breathing in the crisp, fresh air, and if she listened carefully, she was sure she could hear the sea in the distance, dashing against the rocks. James had a truly wonderful home, in a perfect setting.

She showered quickly, washing her hair, and then wrapped herself in a clean, white towelling robe that she found in the airing cupboard. She'd washed her under-wear and cotton top, and left them on the heated towel rail to dry. They wouldn't need ironing, and within an hour or two they should be ready for her to put back on.

There was a hairdryer in a drawer in the bedroom, and she sat for a few minutes at the dressing table, blow-drying her long hair.

James was in the room next door, he'd said, so she sought out the other two guest rooms and looked in on the children. They were both fast asleep, Rosie, pink cheeked, her arms flung out on the duvet, Sam curled up under his covers, with only his nose peeping out.

She smiled, and quietly left them, making her way downstairs. To her surprise, James was in the kitchen.

'I didn't realise you were up,' she said. 'I thought it was early.'

'It is.' His gaze seemed transfixed on her for a moment, and she wondered belatedly if it had been a mistake to come downstairs wearing just a towelling robe. It fitted to just below her knees, but there was still a good expanse of her legs showing. She pulled the robe a little more closely around her.

'I hope you don't mind. I showered and washed my clothes through.'

His gaze wandered over her hair, the rich chestnut tresses spilling over her shoulders in a silken swathe. 'No...uh...um...' He seemed to be having trouble with his voice, and he cleared his throat. 'Not at all. I... uh... I'm an early riser. And I thought I'd make a start on breakfast. I'm sure you must be hungry, after you missed out on supper.'

'I'm starving,' she admitted.

'Good. You'll be able to tuck in, then.' He seemed to have recovered from whatever was bothering him and waved her to a chair. 'Sit down. There's some fresh tea in the pot. And while you're relaxed, I'll take your blood pressure again.'

'Oh, there's really no need for you to do that,' she protested. 'I'm absolutely fine. Having those few hours of sleep did me a world of good.'

'Even so, I just want to be sure.' He fetched a blood-pressure monitor from a cupboard and began to wrap the cuff around her arm.

'How many of these things do you have secreted about the place?' she teased.

'Just one.' A smile hovered on his lips. 'You were pretty much in a state of collapse yesterday, so I dashed down here to grab this machine.' The monitor beeped and he checked the reading. 'That's great,' he said. 'Back to normal. Like I said, it must have happened because you'd been overdoing things.'

'I knew it would be all right.' She gave a rueful smile. 'Anyway, it wouldn't go down too well if a doctor couldn't stand up to a little pressure, would it?'

'There are different kinds of stress,' he pointed out, putting the monitor back in the cupboard. 'As I said before, you haven't really had time to come to terms with your father's death, as well as the worry of having to sell his house and find somewhere for you and the children to live. You can't manage on an adrenaline rush for ever. Sooner or later something has to give, and perhaps being able to relax for once led to meltdown.'

'I suppose you could be right.' She poured tea for both of them. 'I'll help you with breakfast. What were you planning on having?'

'I hadn't worked that out yet.' He looked in the fridge.

'I've plenty of eggs, fresh tomatoes, mushrooms, and there's some bacon and gammon, too.'

'How about I whip up an omelette while you make toast?'

He nodded. 'Sounds perfect to me. We'll make a great team.'

He fished pans out of the cupboard and laid slices of bread on the grill pan. 'Is there anything else you need?'

'A whisk? A simple hand-held one will do.'

He frowned, searching through the cutlery drawer until with a flourish he triumphantly produced one. 'One whisk.'

'And a bowl to mix the eggs in.'

'I can do bowls.' He produced a selection and she chose one of them.

'Thanks. I'm all set now. Do you want to put plates to warm?'

They worked in harmony for the next few minutes, and the kitchen soon became filled with the appetising smell of cooked bacon and golden fried mushrooms.

Rosie and Sam appeared as James was buttering toast and setting it out on plates at the table. 'You're just in time,' he said. 'Grub's up.'

'I'm not eating grubs.' Sam pulled a face, and James looked nonplussed for a moment or two.

'Are you sure?' he teased. 'I heard they were really good for you.'

Rosie laughed. 'There are no grubs,' she told Sam. 'It's your favourite—bacon and mushrooms and omelette.' She sniffed the air appreciatively.

'So that's one more dish I've learned to cook,' James said, and Rosie nodded.

'That makes two, then, if you add popcorn to the list.' Rosie gave him a serene smile as she dipped her fork into the fluffy egg, leaving the others to dissolve into laughter.

After breakfast the children went to play in the garden, where they discovered an old swing and a rope ladder tied to a tree. There was a tyre, too, suspended from the sturdy branch of an apple tree, and Sam took to it with relish.

'They seem to be having a good time,' Sarah said happily, watching them through the kitchen window. 'Were those things put up when your grandparents lived here?'

James nodded, coming to stand beside her. His long body brushed against hers, and the warmth coming from him permeated through her towelling robe, bringing a flush of heat to her cheeks. 'My brother and I used to spend hours out there. We had a great time. My grandfather knew how boys needed to burn off energy with lots of outdoor activities, so he made sure we had our very own adventure playground. I renewed the ropes and kept everything as it was because I thought maybe Jonathan's children would enjoy them some day.'

'I'm sure they will. It was thoughtful of you to do that.' She smiled at him. He'd taken a lot of care in renovating this house and making it into a home, and it showed his love of family in the way he'd kept this playground for his niece and nephew. This house and its garden were made for family life, but would they ever be given over to that? Would there come a time when James decided he wanted a wife and children of his own? A small frisson of alarm rippled through her at the thought. How could she bear it if James were to set up home with another woman?

'What is it?' He gave her a quizzical look.

'Nothing...' She faltered. 'I wondered... I don't think I'll ever settle into a relationship. Too much can go wrong, and I'm just not up to coping with that. But it's a shame, because I was thinking that I'd like children of my own one day. I have Sam and Rosie to care for, of course, and they'll always be precious to me, but I would still have liked to have a baby, or babies, at some point.' She sighed. 'Anyway, it wouldn't work—Sam and Rosie wouldn't understand, would they? I'd hate them to feel that they were being pushed out.' She gazed at him, her green eyes troubled.

Perhaps there was something in her expression that tugged at him, because he quickly put his arms around her and drew her close. 'Is that how it felt for you, when your father married again and started a second family?' Her silky hair hung loose about her shoulders, and now he brushed away glossy tendrils that had fallen across her cheek, hiding her face.

'I don't know. I'm not sure quite how I felt about things at the time.' All she could think about just now was that it was really good to be in his arms. He made her feel warm and safe, as though he truly understood and cared about her. 'I loved them from the first...but somehow I began to feel that I was in the way, intruding on their family life. It wasn't anything that was said or done, but I felt a bit like an outsider, looking in. I don't ever want Rosie and Sam to feel like that.'

'I'm sure they won't.' His voice was gentle and re-assuring. 'They think the world of you, and they know how much you love them. I can see it in the way they talk to you and the way they act around you. It says a lot that they're confident enough to make friends and go out there and enjoy being children. Things could have been very different if you hadn't taken on the responsibility of looking after them.'

'Maybe. I want them to be happy.'

He gazed down at her. 'And what do you want for yourself? Don't you deserve a shot at happiness, too? You've worked really hard to get this far—it's no wonder you collapsed yesterday. Perhaps it's time to start thinking about what you want out of life.'

'I have what I want.' It was true. Right now, she was blissfully content simply to be wrapped up in his embrace. She could kid herself that she was cosseted, cherished almost, as his fingers splayed out over her spine and his other hand rested warmly on the curve of her hip. It didn't matter that he was simply comforting her, offering to share her burden.

'Do you?'

She lifted her face to him, and was immediately lost in the intensity of his gaze. 'For now, anyway.'

He shook his head, frowning as though he was battling with himself over something. She couldn't tell what he was thinking. But after a moment or two it seemed to pass, and now flame shimmered in the depths of his eyes and a smile hovered on his lips—lips that were just a breath away from hers. He lowered his head, and heat surged in her as she realised what he was about to do. Her heart lurched inside her chest, and then his lips touched hers, soft and compelling, achingly sweet, leaving a trail of fire in their wake.

A pulse began to throb in her throat, and she wanted to lean into him, to let her soft curves mesh with his hard body, but most of all she wanted him to kiss her again, to want her, to need her and take all she had to offer. She hardly dared believe that he might truly want her. Shakily, she ran her hands up over his chest, curving them around his shoulders and gently kneading the muscular contours with the tips of her fingers.

He sucked in his breath, and then a ragged, shuddery sigh escaped him. His hands moved over her, shaping her, moulding her to him and tracing a path as though he would learn every dip and hollow and commit it to memory. His mouth came down on hers, crushing the softness of her lips, tasting, exploring, and growing ever more passionate as she hungrily returned his kisses. She clung to him, wanting this moment to go on and on.

Then, with shocking suddenness, the kitchen door clattered open and the electric tension in the air was shattered, lost in time as they broke apart and turned to see what had caused the interruption.

'Rosie won't let me go on the swing.' Sam's chin jutted with indignation. 'She's been on it for ages. You have to tell her that it's my turn.' Thankfully, he was so het up about his grievance that he didn't notice there was anything at all wrong with either of them.

Sarah was breathing deeply, trying hard to slow the heavy, thudding beat of her heart. She was in a state of shock, overcome by the realisation that for a while she'd forgotten completely where she was and how she should behave. What was she doing, getting herself involved with James? How many times had she told herself that she must steer clear of any entanglement with him? Was she determined to set herself up for more hurt?

'Tell her she has five more minutes,' she said, pulling in a deep breath and finding her voice, 'and then you must swap over. I'll let you know when the time's up.'

'Wha-a-t? That's not fair!' Clearly, he wasn't happy with the five-minutes rule, but Sarah was in no mood for a drawn-out discussion.

'You heard what I said.'

Sam went out again, muttering to himself, and a moment later they heard him shout triumphantly, 'Five minutes, then you've gotta give me a go or you're in big trouble. Sarah says so.'

James looked at her. He was frowning, and she guessed he was as troubled as she was. 'Sarah, I...'

'It's all right.' She shook her head. 'It's just as well he came in. We were both carried away there for a while. It's been a strange couple of days. I don't think either of us is thinking straight.'

His expression was sober. 'I don't want to hurt you, or cause you any more problems. The truth is I wasn't thinking at all.'

'No...well, it doesn't matter.' Perhaps he'd discovered that she wasn't a skinny teenager any more, and being a red-blooded male he'd been carried away with the heat of the moment. It hadn't meant anything to him...nothing of any importance, at any rate...and that was why he'd said he didn't want to hurt her. 'Let's forget it happened, shall we?' She was giving him a get-out clause.

'Okay. If you say so.' His voice was ragged.

He took them home a couple of hours later, and spent time finishing off the fireplaces with the black grate polish, while Sarah caught up on chores and Rosie and Sam went to play with the children next door.

'I'll have a go at sanding the floorboards downstairs another time, if you like,' he offered when she went to admire his handiwork a little later. The fireplaces looked magnificent, as good as new, and she really appreciated the work he had done.

'You've done a great job,' she said. 'I can't ask you to do any more. I've already asked too much of you. And I don't want you to feel obliged to help me out. I can manage, I'm sure. It takes time, that's all.'

'It's not a problem. Like I said, I'm interested in renovation...it's good to see a property fulfil its potential, and these floors are basically sound. They need a bit of care, that's all. And I have a machine that will do the job in no time at all.'

She smiled. 'Okay, then. Thanks. For everything.'

He nodded. 'I'd better go.' His grey gaze slanted over her. 'I'll see you at work tomorrow.'

'At the air ambulance station, yes.' She looked forward to those days that were spent out of the hospital, attending to on-the-spot emergencies. They weren't good for anyone unfortunate enough to be involved in an accident, or to be taken ill suddenly, of course, but from a professional point of view it was good to know that they could give immediate lifesaving help in that first all-important golden hour.

She went with him to the door and watched him slide into the driver's seat of his car. He hadn't made any attempt to touch her since Sam had burst into his kitchen, and while she was glad of that, she was sad about it, too.

She was mixed up inside, emotionally vulnerable, and at a loss to know how to deal with her feelings.

James didn't appear to be having any problems on that score. Kissing her had been a momentary lapse and now he was back to his normal self, confident, energetic and ready to move on. It would take her a little longer to get there.

In the morning, she was at the air ambulance base when the first call came in. 'Okay, it looks as though we're on our own on this one,' Tom, the pilot, said. 'James is still attending an incident that came in an hour ago. It was only a couple of miles away, so he took the rapid-response car. The paramedics wanted a doctor on the scene.'

'Do you think you can handle this without him?' the co-pilot asked as they scrambled for the helicopter. 'An ambulance is on its way to the scene, but apparently it's been held up.' Alex frowned, running a hand through his wavy, brown hair. His hazel eyes were concerned.

'I'll be absolutely fine, Alex,' she said quickly. 'You don't have to worry. I won't let anyone down.'

'Sorry, Doc.' Tom looked embarrassed. 'Alex worries about all the new people who join the crew. It's not meant to be a personal criticism—but we were hoping James would be back before we took off.'

They were airborne within a couple of minutes, and Sarah concentrated on finding out all she could about the incident they were about to attend.

'It's a ten-year-old boy who has fallen down a mine shaft,' Alex told her. 'An old copper mine, apparently. They're dotted all around the area. Trouble was, they were closed down decades ago, and when they were abandoned the entrances to the shafts were covered with timber and soil. I think, over the years, the timbers have begun to rot, and every now and again they cave in.'

'That's awful,' Sarah said, her heart going out to the child who had unwittingly been swallowed up into a deep chasm in the ground. 'I can't believe that no one's taken responsibility for them.' She thought about the child lying at the bottom of the shaft, cold and most likely wet, too. He was the same age as Sam. 'Are his parents at the mine, do we know?'

Alex shook his head. 'He was with his older brother when it happened. The police have been trying to find his parents, but they're not at home.'

They flew over heath, covered with mauve heather and yellow gorse, and soon the helicopter landed in a safe area close by the mine. Police and fire crew were already there, and Sarah was beginning to see why Alex might have been worried about her working on this venture. Someone would have to go down into that mine shaft to rescue the child. It was more than likely he was badly injured after such a fall, and was probably suffering from broken limbs—if he was still alive. That new anxiety struck her forcibly.

'Has he been talking?' she asked one of the fire crew. 'Has anyone been able to speak to him?'

'He's said a few words…nothing much, nothing intelligible, anyway.'

That could mean he was semi-conscious, making it all the more important that he have medical attention as soon as possible. 'I can see you have the winch in place. I'll need to get into a harness to go down to him. Will you help me with that?'

'Are you sure you're up to it?' The man gave her a doubtful look. 'It can be dangerous going down into these shafts. There could be loose timbers, rock falls—perhaps it would be better if you gave instructions to one of our crew. He'll tell you how the boy is doing, and you could maybe tell him how to go on from there.'

She shook her head. 'I can't see that working. Your fireman might not be able to take precautions against spinal or pelvic injury, and I doubt he'll know how to give injections or set up a fluid line. You need a medic down there.' She started to walk towards the winch. 'Will you help me get set up?'

Reluctantly, he did as she asked. The harness was designed to fit snugly around the person, and there were lots of buckles to be fastened and checked. It was imperative that everything be fixed in place so as to be perfectly secure.

'What's going on here?'

Sarah had started to climb into the harness when James's voice cracked through the air like a whip. She looked up at him, startled to see his face etched in taut lines, his mouth flat, compressed.

'I'm going down into the shaft to look after the boy,' she said. 'His name's Ross. He's fallen about twenty feet into a cavern and might be semi-conscious.' She gave him a brief smile. 'I'm glad you made it here after all.'

'So am I. Step out of the harness, please, Sarah. I'll go down in your place.'

She stared at him in disbelief. 'But I'm all ready to go.'

'Not any more. This is way too risky for you.'

Affronted, she tilted her chin, and said firmly, 'For you, too, I'd have thought. I've had a lot of rock-climbing experience. I'm quite prepared to go down there and see to the boy. I don't see it as a problem.'

'You may not, but I'm afraid I do. Rock climbing is not the same as caving or potholing, and I have experience in both of those, so I'll go in your place. Step out of the way, Sarah, please.'

Everything in her told her that she must stand her ground, but she was all too conscious of time passing while they argued, with danger to the boy increasing with every minute. Neither did she want to create a scene in front of the police and fire crew, so she said in a low, exasperated voice, 'What gives you the right to stop me?'

'Seniority.'

She gave him a furious glare and finally stood to one side, leaving him to get into the harness. How could he do this to her? What had possessed him to play the seniority card like that, when she was perfectly capable of going down that shaft?

He had his medical kit with him, and she handed him a torch. 'It'll be pitch black in there,' she said.

'I know. Thanks.'

All she could do now was watch and wait while James descended the shaft, followed by one of the fire crew. It was galling to have to stand there and do nothing.

After several minutes a stretcher was lowered down, and more time passed before James indicated that they were ready to come back up. The firemen began to winch up the stretcher, and slowly hauled the boy to safety.

'How's he doing?' Sarah asked as soon as James came to the surface. She was still smarting at his treatment of her, but her focus had to be on the child.

'He has rib and pelvis fractures,' he answered quietly. 'He's not doing too well at all, I'm afraid. I think there must be massive internal bleeding. His blood pressure is falling and his heart rate's rapid.' James hesitated briefly, and she could see that he was acutely disturbed by this young boy's condition. Now that the child had been brought to the surface, he set about finding intravenous access and began to put in a fluid line to help resuscitate him. 'I'm worried that he might go into shock, so we have to get him to hospital as soon as possible. I've given him painkillers and stabilised the fracture with a pelvic sling, so that should compress the area and stop some of the bleeding.'

Sarah knelt down beside the stretcher. 'He's struggling to breathe,' she said in an urgent, low voice, glancing at James. The boy was being given oxygen through a mask, but it obviously wasn't sufficient to help him. 'His condition's deteriorating rapidly.' She studied the rise and fall of his chest and said quickly, 'Something's not right. There's a segment of his ribcage that's not moving in tune with the rest.' She frowned. 'There must be several rib fractures—part of the ribcage has broken and become detached.'

He winced. He had the fluid line in place now. 'A flail chest,' he said in a low tone. 'I suspected as much, but it was too dark down there to see properly.'

Sarah quickly examined the boy, who was lying mo-

tionless but groaning in pain. 'I know this must be uncomfortable for you, Ross,' she said softly, 'but we'll
look after you and help you to feel better. It won't be
too long before we have you in hospital.'

She turned back to James. 'His windpipe has devi-
ated to one side and his neck veins are distended. One
of the ribs must have pierced his lung.' This was more
bad news. It meant that air was collecting in the pleu-
ral cavity and had nowhere to escape. As it built up, it
was disrupting other organs and tissues. 'We have to
act quickly.' If they didn't act promptly to do something
about it, the child could go into cardiac arrest and they
might lose him.

He nodded. 'I'm on it.' He reached for equipment
from his medical pack and then carefully injected anaesthetic between the boy's ribs. Then he made an inci-
sion in the chest wall and slid a catheter in place. There
was a satisfying hiss as trapped air escaped, and Sarah
sealed off the end of the tube in a water-filled bottle
that acted as a one-way valve.

'Okay, I've taped the tube in place.' He glanced at
her. 'I'll stabilise the flail segment with a gauze pad
and then we can be on our way.'

'Good.' She didn't say any more. She was too annoyed with him to speak to him about anything other
than work, and her only concern at that moment was
that Ross needed to be transported to the hospital in a
matter of minutes. By the time he was there, perhaps
his parents would have been located and would be in
time to visit him and reassure him before he went to
Theatre for lifesaving surgery.

They loaded Ross into the bay of the helicopter and

within a couple of minutes they were on their way. The
ambulance still had not arrived, and Alex told her it had
been held up by a road-traffic accident that had happened while they'd been on their way to the mine. She
absorbed the news with a sombre expression. Without
medical intervention, it was doubtful Ross would have
been alive by the time the paramedics arrived. This
way, he at least had a chance of survival.

Once they were at the hospital they handed Ross over
to the trauma team, who whisked him away. His parents were there, waiting for him, and Sarah breathed a
faint sigh of relief as his anxious mother hurried forward to hold his hand.

She walked back to the helicopter without looking
at James. She held her head high, ready to deal with
Tom's and Alex's comments. They were all too aware
that James had set her to one side like a spare part.

Strangely, though, they were quiet on the subject.
Were they on her side? Or did they think that, as a
woman, she shouldn't be taking on such risks? It was
such an old-fashioned viewpoint.

James had no such inhibitions. 'I was horrified when
I saw you getting ready to go down into that mine,'
he said as they took their seats on the helicopter. 'All
I could think about was the danger you were putting
yourself in.'

'You didn't seem to have any qualms about going
down,' she answered in a terse voice. 'And from the
looks of things, you didn't come out of it unscathed.'
Now that she had the chance to look at him properly,
she saw that he had a deep gash on his forehead, hidden for the most part by an unruly lock of dark hair.

There was a graze on his hand, too, she noticed, when he pulled on the seat belt and fastened it in place. 'If I'd been allowed to do my job and go down, I would have accepted injuries as one of the hazards.'

'And that's okay, is it, to risk your life in the course of the job?'

Her eyes widened in astonishment. 'Why on earth should that be all right for you and not for me?' she demanded.

'I'm not the one with a family to care for,' he said bluntly. 'I shudder to think what might have happened to you. What do you imagine will happen to Sam and Rosie if you're injured or worse? How will they react if anything bad happens to you? Who will look after them? Haven't they suffered enough? Surely you can't think purely of yourself now, if you really mean to act as a permanent guardian to them?'

She was stunned by what he said. It was true she hadn't thought beyond helping the boy, but what would he have her do? This was her job, and if he weren't around, wouldn't she do the same again?

He was right about Rosie and Sam, though. If she was serious about taking care of them, she had to rethink her priorities. It troubled her deeply, thinking about that. Perhaps, on the face of it, he'd had good reason to step in and take over, but the intrusion still needled her. He'd pulled rank, and that annoyed her intensely.

CHAPTER SIX

'How is Ross doing?' Sarah asked the specialist nurse in charge of the paediatric intensive care unit. 'The poor child was in a really bad way yesterday. I couldn't bring myself to start work without coming here to check up on him first.'

'He's still in a critical condition, I'm afraid.' The nurse gave her a sympathetic smile. 'It was dreadful, what happened to him. His parents have been beside themselves with worry and I've had to send them down to the cafeteria to take a break. Otherwise, I don't think they would have eaten since yesterday.' She frowned. 'I doubt he would have survived if it hadn't been for you and Dr Benson. But the good news is he had surgery on his pelvis yesterday, almost immediately after you brought him into A and E. Mr Norris managed to stop the bleeding, but of course the lad had lost a lot of blood already.'

Sarah nodded and looked down at the white-faced child lying in the hospital bed. There were drips and tubes taped in place so that he could receive lifesaving fluids, oxygen and medication, and where his broken pelvis had been treated there were post-operative surgical drains.

His blood pressure was still low and his heart rate fluctuated as she watched the monitors.

'On top of everything else, he was dreadfully cold when he arrived here,' the nurse told her. 'We were all very worried about him.'

'I know you're taking good care of him,' Sarah told her. 'We can't do anything more but wait now to see what happens.'

'Mmm. He doesn't look very strong to start with, does he?' The nurse gave Ross one last look before excusing herself to go and see to another patient.

Sarah stood by the bedside for a while longer. 'You have to get better, Ross,' she urged. 'Be strong. You can do it.'

There was a movement beside her, and she looked around to see that James had come to join her. She might have known that he would come to see how the boy was getting on. They were in tune when it came to how they felt about their patients. She checked him out surreptitiously and, as ever, when he was at work, he was immaculately dressed in a dark grey suit, with the jacket open, showing a pristine shirt and soft blue-grey tie.

'You're obviously worried about him,' he said, 'but from what I heard, the surgery went well, and they've done X-rays of his chest to show that the chest tube is in the right place. They're giving him strong painkilling medication at the moment, so hopefully his breathing will be more comfortable.'

'Yes, it looks as though they're doing everything they can for him.' Her expression was rueful. 'I can't help feeling particularly involved with this young lad.

Looking at him, it feels as though time's going backwards.' She sighed, thinking of what had happened some time ago. 'It was a boy like Ross that caused me to take up medicine in the first place.'

'Really?' He studied her thoughtfully, his dark brows lifting a fraction in query. 'What happened?'

'I was on a rock-climbing weekend with Murray when we heard a shout. A moment later we saw a boy come tumbling down the cliff face near where we were. I think he must have climbed over the safety fence then lost his footing and slipped over the edge. We called out the emergency services, and started to go back down the cliff to where he had landed on an outcrop.'

Even now, it was distressing to think back to that worrying time. 'He'd broken his arm, and his foot was at a weird angle to his leg. Murray used dressing pads from his emergency first-aid kit to stem the bleeding, and we splinted his limbs as best we could using tape from the pack. I was glad we were there for him because he would have been terrified if he'd been on his own. At least we were able to comfort and reassure him, otherwise I don't know how long he would have lain there before anyone found him.'

'It was a good thing you knew what to do.'

She winced. 'It was Murray who knew what to do. He'd done a first-aid course because as a climber he was worried about these sorts of situations cropping up. It made me think seriously about doing a course myself, but in the end I decided to go in for medicine instead.'

He smiled. 'There's a huge amount of difference between those two choices. For what it's worth, I think you made a good decision.'

'Yes.' She gave a wry smile. 'Contrary to popular opinion, I did manage to make one or two back then.' She said it in a droll tone, and he sent her a quick glance.

'I'll hazard a guess that you're still annoyed over what happened yesterday. Would I be right?'

'You could say that.' She flashed him a sparking glance. 'Annoyed is such a mild word, don't you think?' She moved away from the bedside. 'You undermined me in public and stopped me from doing my job. You were way out of line.'

'I did what I thought was right.'

'Of course you did.' Her mouth made a flat line. 'Anyway, I don't want to talk about that now. I'm a few minutes early and I want to go and look through the lab results before I start my shift on A and E.'

'I'll come with you.'

'Fine.' She didn't say any more, and responded to his conversation with brief one-word answers. The more she thought about it, the more she resented his actions.

Once they were in the A and E unit, she went over to the central desk and looked through the wire tray for lab and radiology reports. 'There's an update here on Nicola Carter,' she told him, glancing through the patient's file. 'It's no wonder she suffered an adrenal crisis. The radiologist's report says she has a tumour on the pituitary gland.'

His mouth made a downward turn. 'We'd better get the endocrinologist to take a look at her,' he said. 'Let's go and bring these scans up on the computer.'

They went into the annexe, and brought up the patient's notes on screen, but Gemma, the triage nurse, came looking for them a moment later. 'There's someone asking to see you, Sarah. He says he's Rachel Veasey's brother, Harry. I've shown him to the relatives' waiting room.'

'Oh, brilliant. Thanks, Gemma. I'm glad we managed to find him.'

'You're welcome.' Gemma walked away, in a hurry to see to incoming patients.

'How did that come about?' James asked with a frown. 'This is the girl who collapsed through drink and drugs, isn't it? I thought she didn't have any family.'

'She told me she had a brother, and her friends said they thought he was living in a village in Somerset, so I tried to track him down. I thought he might be on the electoral register, and when I looked I found there weren't that many Veaseys listed, so I took a chance and contacted one of them. I wrote to him.' Her mouth curved with pleasure. 'It seems I might have been lucky and managed to find the right person.'

'You went to a lot of trouble to get in touch with him.' He studied her curiously. 'Is this because you feel the need to bring families together?'

'I suppose it must be. I think Rachel needs someone from her family to care about her. There was a void, and I wanted to fill it.'

'Because you can't fill the void in your own life?'

She pulled in a deep breath. His calm, penetrating assessment shocked her. 'Maybe.' She shrugged awkwardly. 'I know you don't think it's a good idea, but I've never given up on finding my mother. I want to know why she walked out, and the question keeps eating away at me. I feel as though I can't move on until I have an answer. I can't settle. I can't get my life in order.' She ran a hand through her hair. 'The card I had from her last Christmas was postmarked London, but I just don't seem to be able to track her down.'

'It would surely be easier for her to get in touch with you? She probably doesn't want to be found—I can't help thinking you're laying yourself open for trouble if you insist on looking for her.'

'That's as may be. I'm still determined to try.'

He smiled wryly. 'I guessed that might be the case.' He was pensive for a moment or two. 'It's possible she could have remarried, I suppose. Maybe you need to get in touch with the General Register Office and see if you can track down a marriage using her maiden name. Hopefully, that will give you her new name.'

She blinked, looking at him in stunned surprise. 'Oh, wow! You're right, of course. Why on earth didn't I think of that?'

He smiled, his head tilting slightly to one side as he studied her. 'Perhaps because you're too close to the problem?'

'Yes, I see that.' Her green eyes were wide, shimmering with a sudden film of joyful tears. 'Thanks, James,' she said huskily. She was so overwhelmed by the significance of this new idea that she wrapped her arms around him and gave him a hug. 'I absolutely forgive you for everything. You're a genius.' She lifted her face to him, ready to plant a swift kiss on his cheek, but at that moment he turned his head and their lips met in a soft collision. She heard his sharp intake of breath, and tension sparked like a flash of wildfire between them.

There was an instant of complete stillness and then, with a muffled groan, he pulled her to him, covering her mouth with his. He kissed her hard, a deep, fervent kiss that caught her off balance so that she clung to him, revelling in this exhilarating, heat-filled moment.

Almost as soon as it had begun, though, it was over. James lifted his head and held her at arm's length as though he needed space but was reluctant to let her go completely. The air between them was thick with un-bidden yearning. His breathing was ragged, coming in short bursts, and Sarah stared at him, her whole body feverish from that brief, close encounter.

His features were taut, and his eyes were dark and troubled. 'I shouldn't have done that,' he said in a rough-ened voice. 'I mustn't do that. I'm your boss. You're on a probationary three months and it isn't right. It isn't a professional way for me to behave. I'm sorry.'

Sarah's throat was suddenly dry and she swallowed carefully. 'It was my fault. You shouldn't blame yourself. I was carried away by the heat of the moment, thinking I might be able to get in touch with my mother after all this time. I shouldn't have flung myself at you.' The ethics of the situation didn't seem relevant to her—after all, she was a qualified doctor, not a student in training, but it obviously bothered James, and she wasn't going to try to persuade him otherwise. Perhaps he was looking for an excuse to keep away from her. She had no real idea what made him tick as far as she was con-cerned. Maybe he was as confused as she was.

He released his hold on her and she moved away from him, not knowing what else to do or what to say. 'I'll...I'll go and talk to Harry, and then I'd better see who Gemma has lined up waiting for me.'

'Okay.'

She made a hurried escape. Her heart was still thudding from the intensity of that kiss, but the whole episode puzzled her. What did James really feel for her? He clearly wanted her, but was it just a whim, a passing fancy, a fleeting passion? The whole thing was bewildering.

She spoke to Harry for a few minutes and then took him to Rachel's ward. The young girl was still thin and pale looking, and she was very tired, probably as a result of the irregular heart rhythm she was suffering as a result of her use of Ecstasy. Sarah checked her notes, satisfying herself that everything was being done to help her to recover.

'Harry?' Rachel's face lit up with pleasure. 'You're here… I didn't think… Oh, I'm so glad to see you.'

'Me, too.' Harry pulled up a chair and sat down at his sister's bedside, and Sarah decided it was time to leave the two of them to talk to one another in private.

'I'll be in A and E if you need me,' she told Harry. She wrote her phone number down on a scrap of paper and handed it to him. 'Here's my number in case you want to talk to me or if there's anything I can do to help your sister.'

He thanked her, and she went back to the emergency department, feeling lighter at heart now that Rachel had someone dear to her close by.

'There's a girl waiting to be seen in the treatment room,' Gemma told her a minute or so later. 'She's twenty years old. A friend called the ambulance. Apparently she passed out a couple of times and was out of it for a while. The paramedics said her blood pressure and pulse were both low. She just had a break-up with her boyfriend, so the friend thinks it might be something to do with that…an emotional reaction.'

'I'll look at her and see if we can find out what's happening. Thanks, Gemma.' Sarah went to the treatment room and introduced herself to the young woman who was waiting for her there. She was a pretty girl, blonde with blue eyes and a slender, shapely figure. She told Sarah that her friend had gone to get them both a coffee from the machine.

'Okay, Ann-Marie, do you want to tell me what happened?'

'I collapsed,' the girl told her. She was pale, and her eyes were red rimmed as though she'd been crying. 'I felt really strange all at once, and it was as though I couldn't breathe. I was dizzy and light-headed.'

'Did you have breakfast this morning?'

'Yes, I had a bowl of cereal.'

Sarah smiled. 'That's good. You're not watching your weight, or anything like that?'

Ann-Marie shook her head. 'No, not at all.'

'So, did anything happen just before you started to feel this way—a bang on the head or has something out of the ordinary happened recently?'

This met with another shake of the head, but Ann-Marie added huskily, 'I had a text from my boyfriend. He wants us to break up…says things aren't working out.' Tears welled up in her eyes and she sniffed and dabbed at them with a tissue. 'It upset me, and after that I started to feel strange. It was as though everything drained out of me.' She hesitated. 'It's not the first time I've fainted, though…so I'm not really sure if it's the break-up that made me ill.'

'It must be distressing for you, but try not to upset yourself.' Sarah brought her stethoscope from her pocket. 'I'll examine you, if I may, and see if we can find out what's wrong.'

The examination didn't reveal anything untoward, but Sarah said quietly, 'That all seems to be okay, but I think we'll admit you to our observation ward so that we can run some tests and keep an eye on you for a while. I'll ask the nurse to set up an ECG to monitor your heart rate and exclude any problems there.'

She made the arrangements and went to see the rest of the patients on her list. Some time later, when she was treating a man suffering from an asthma attack, James came to find her and drew her to one side.

'Keep him on the nebulised salbutamol for the time being,' she told the nurse, 'and let me know if there's any change in his condition.' She left the room with James.

'Is something wrong?' she asked. She saw he had Ann-Marie's file in his hand.

'Gemma tells me you've admitted this woman to the observation ward,' he said. 'We've quite a high number of admissions already and I'm wondering if it's really necessary to keep her here. After all, her symptoms are probably something her GP could deal with... they could even have a purely emotional basis. Perhaps she's overwrought and not coping too well with her love life. That's not strictly something we should be dealing with here.'

'That's all possibly true, but something's bothering me. I have an instinct about her.' Sarah was on the defensive. 'She said it had happened before, and I want to get to the bottom of it. She was in a state of collapse when the paramedics picked her up, and I'd sooner we were on hand to deal with the situation if it happens again.'

'All right. But if she's stable in the morning, you should send her home with a letter for her GP.'

She nodded. 'I will.' At least he hadn't overridden her decision, and she was glad about that. She might be wrong about Ann-Marie, but it was a case of better safe than sorry as far as she was concerned.

James glanced at her as she started to walk back towards the treatment room. 'If it's all right with you, I could come round to your place to start on the floors after work today. I know you're always busy with one thing and another, but I won't get in your way. I've hunted through the mountains of stuff in the outbuildings and found the sanding machine, so it should make fairly light work of them.'

'You don't need to do that,' she said quickly. After what kept happening between them, perhaps it would be for the best if she avoided any more contact with him outside work. Going on as they were was surely like playing with fire? Sooner or later, she'd find her fingers were burned.

'I know that, but I'd like to get to work on them. It's very satisfying, seeing things restored to their former glory. Will you be at home?'

'Yes.' She frowned, searching for excuses. She didn't want to be blunt and tell him to stay away, but everything in her was telling her she needed to steer clear of him away from work. 'I'll be very busy, though, working on the internet article for next week's topic.

And I promised Rosie and Sam I'd take them to the local library to choose some books. So, you see, you could be making a wasted journey and I don't want to put you out. You really don't need to worry. I'll get around to doing the floors myself some time. My priority right now is to get the roof repaired, and I've made an appointment for a roofing company to send someone round.'

'Yes, I can see that's important. It might not be too big a job, though. Let's hope so, anyway.' He didn't say any more, and she hoped he'd taken the hint. It was a relief. It would surely be far better if they kept their work and private lives separate from now on.

The rest of the day flew by as she dealt with a steady stream of patients and by the time she went home and picked up the children from Murray's house, she was more than ready for a break. Sam was unusually subdued, she noticed, but Murray didn't have any clue what that was all about.

'He hasn't said anything to me, except that he has to get some information together for a school project. He's supposed to present it to the class some time next week and he hasn't made a start yet, apparently.'

Sarah's expression was rueful. 'Perhaps it's just as well we're making a trip to the library, then. With any luck he might find something there to inspire him.'

They arrived back at the house some time later, armed with several colourful books, and Sarah began to prepare supper while the children disappeared into their rooms. Murray came round to collect a book she'd picked up for him, and she invited him to stay and eat with them.

'It's nothing much, just a casserole. I put all the ingredients together this morning and set the automatic timer, so it should be ready any time now.'

'It smells wonderful,' Murray said, sniffing the air, and when she served up the meal a short time later, they all ate appreciatively.

Sam was still morose, not saying very much, and Sarah tried to wheedle out of him what was wrong, while she stacked crockery in the dishwasher, but it was no use. He wasn't talking.

Then the doorbell rang and Murray went to answer it. He came back a moment later, saying, 'You have a visitor.'

She looked up, and was startled to see James standing next to him. 'James? I hadn't expected— So you decided to come after all?'

'I did. After all, you didn't expressly tell me not to come.' He glanced at Murray and then looked back at Sarah. 'I hope I'm not intruding on anything. I can always leave.'

'No...no, not at all. You're welcome to stay.'

'I'd better be going, anyway,' Murray said. 'Thanks for the meal, Sarah. It was delicious. I'll return the favour some time.'

'I'm glad you enjoyed it.' She went with him to the kitchen door, waving him off.

'You and he must spend quite a bit of time together, with him living next door,' James said speculatively, his dark eyes narrowed. 'You seem to get along very well with one another.'

'We do.' She looked at him fleetingly, not wanting to dwell too long on his powerfully masculine frame, made all the more impressive by the clothes he was wearing. Dark jeans moulded themselves to his strong, muscular legs, and a T-shirt hugged the contours of his chest. 'I see you've brought the sanding machine with you,' she said. 'You must mean business.'

'If that's all right with you?'

'I... Yes, of course. I haven't cleared any of the furniture out, though. I was pretty sure you wouldn't be coming.'

'That's not a problem. I'll see to it.'

Rosie had stayed quiet so far, but now she looked carefully at the machine. 'What's that for?' she asked.

'It's for getting all the old dirt and sealant off the wooden floorboards so that they come up looking clean and new,' James told her. 'Then, when that's done, they can be sealed again with polyurethane to give them a fine sheen.'

'That'll be good,' she said approvingly. 'They look old and grotty now, don't they?' She smiled. 'I can help you move the furniture if you like. Do you think you might start with the dining room?'

'That sounds like a good idea, though I don't want you hurting yourself moving furniture.' He glanced at Sarah. 'Is it all right with you if I start in the dining room? What do you think?'

'Yes, that's okay.' She glanced at Sam, conscious of how quiet he was being. 'Perhaps you'd like to help us get the furniture out of the room, Sam?'

Sam lifted his shoulders but didn't make any attempt to answer, and James said in a sympathetic tone, 'Are you all right, Sam? You're not saying very much, and that's not like you at all. Is everything okay?'

Sam pressed his lips together and seemed to be thinking hard about something. Then he looked at Sarah and said, 'If you're doing the floors, does that mean we're staying here, or are you making the house look good so you can sell it?'

'Heavens, where did that thought come from?' She looked at him in surprise. 'What makes you think we would be leaving? Is that what's been troubling you these last few hours?'

'Ricky Morton says we're not a proper family—you're not our mum, he says, and we don't have a dad. And he says if you get fed up of looking after us we won't have anybody and we'll have to go into care. Then you can sell the house and get somewhere just for you.'

Sarah reeled back from that as though she'd been kicked in the stomach. It took her breath away momentarily and she struggled to get herself together again. 'That's an awful lot of guesswork from Ricky,' she said at last. She was still shocked and flummoxed by Sam's innocent outburst. 'Why on earth would I get fed up with looking after you?' Sarah hugged him close to her, shocked that he could even think such a thing. Rosie came and huddled next to her and she put a protective arm around each of them.

'It seems to me Ricky's saying an awful lot of things that he doesn't really understand,' she said carefully. 'He's wrong. Perhaps he has problems of his own that make him think that way, but it isn't going to happen. I'll always want to take care of you.'

Sam gazed up at her, his expression earnest and pleading at the same time. 'Do you promise?'

'I promise, Sam. I love both of you, and we can be a

family, the three of us. There are lots of families where there's only one parent.' She looked at James and saw that he was frowning. 'Isn't that true, James?' she said, willing him to back her up in this.

'It is,' he responded, 'and things often work out very well for them.' He hesitated for a moment, and then went down on his haunches by the children and said carefully, 'I think you're very lucky to have Sarah taking care of you. She's changed her life so that the three of you can be together. And as to making the house look good, she's doing it because she can see it's a solid house with big rooms and she wants it to be perfect for you.'

Sam slowly nodded. 'I was scared. Mum and Dad went away, and I don't want Sarah to do the same.'

'I don't ever want to go away,' Sarah told him softly, bending to kiss him lightly on the forehead. She hugged them both tight. 'Everything I'm doing, I'm doing for both of you.'

'And that means making a start on the dining-room floor,' James said, standing up. 'Do I have some helpers?'

'Sarah and I can move the chairs,' Rosie decided, already on her way out of the kitchen.

'Can I have a go with the sander?' Sam wanted to know.

Some half an hour later James was ready to make a start, and after Sam made a few forays with the machine alongside the wall where the cupboards used to stand, the children disappeared upstairs to play in their rooms. There was half an hour left before bedtime and Sarah advised them to make the most of it. Two minutes later an argument erupted between them as Sam tried to muscle in on Rosie's computer game, and Sarah had to go and sort things out.

She came downstairs a short time later and made coffee. 'It was difficult earlier,' she said, offering James a cup, 'finding the right thing to say to Sam. I know they worry, and I do what I can to reassure them, but I can't promise them that everything will go smoothly. You were right about me taking risks going down the mine shaft, but I didn't want to admit it. Sometimes, when it's called for, we have to do what we think is the right thing. And it seemed that way to me at the time. If I had to choose between taking a chance on saving that boy's life or doing nothing, I'd take a chance, without even thinking about it. It doesn't mean I don't care about Rosie and Sam.'

He swallowed some of the hot liquid and set his cup down on the mantelpiece. 'I know that. The truth is, when I saw you getting ready to be lowered down into that pit, I was shocked at the thought of what might happen to you. It overrode my better judgement, if you like. If it had been anyone else, I'd probably have suggested that I go down into the mine alongside him or her, but with you, somehow, it's different. Perhaps I was wrong, but I can't say that I wouldn't do exactly the same thing if those circumstances arose again.'

Her jaw dropped a fraction. He'd done it because he cared about her and hadn't wanted to see her heading into danger. Her heart made a tentative leap within her chest. He cared about her and wanted to keep her safe. That was more than she could ever have hoped for. Even so, for her own sake, she knew she mustn't read too much into it.

She gave a rueful smile. 'I have to make choices and face the consequences, and I have to do it on my own. You're a caring, thoughtful person, but it isn't right that you should have to worry about my wellbeing.'

His mouth twisted. 'I don't think it works quite that way.'

'No?' She sent him a quizzical glance. 'I accept I have responsibilities now. I have to look out for Rosie and Sam, and I'm doing it the best way I can. I'm really glad you backed me up earlier…it helped a lot. It made me feel better, and I could see the children were reassured, too.'

'I'm pleased about that, too.' He frowned. 'It's difficult looking after children, isn't it? They can be quite a handful. It's not just a question of sorting out fights at school, or stopping them from rolling about in mud at the zoo…there are all these undercurrents going on as well, not to mention the everyday problems of getting them to where they need to be and keeping them from laying into one another.' He brooded on that for a few seconds. 'It must have been difficult for you…but you seem to have the perfect temperament for it.'

'I don't know about that. I've not really had a choice.' She sipped her coffee, watching him over the rim of her cup. 'I've had to learn how to do things. I'm still learning.'

'Yeah.' He smiled and reached for the sanding machine. 'It's a hard lesson, but you seem to be handling it pretty well. I'm amazed by the way you've got to grips with everything and turned your life around. You should be proud of yourself.'

He started up the sander and set to work, and Sarah

stood by, watching him for a while, enjoying the way he moved, at one with the machine, making calm, steady inroads into the years of accumulated grime that had discoloured the wooden floorboards. Then she wandered away, going back into the kitchen and switching on her computer so that she could start work on her internet article.

Her fingers hovered aimlessly over the keyboard. James obviously felt something for her, or why would he be looking out for her? And he wanted her…when she was in his arms his kisses left her in no doubt of that. Despite his misgivings, she was certain he wanted more, and this time she wasn't a naïve seventeen-year-old. She was a woman, and if she pushed things, she was pretty sure his resolve would melt like snow in the sunshine.

But that didn't mean he was ready for anything other than a heady affair, did it? And even if he was, how could they ever have a future together when she was so uncertain about the steadfastness of relationships? Hadn't her own mother abandoned her? Why should James be any different? She couldn't bear it if one day he chose to turn his back on her.

CHAPTER SEVEN

'HEY, look at you! You're doing really well, young Ross. It's great to see you out and about. Last time I saw you, you were flat on your back in Intensive Care.' James gave the boy a beaming smile, watching as his mother pushed him in a wheelchair into the emergency department. She came to a halt by the central desk, and James exchanged a few words with her before turning his attention back to her son. 'You're looking so much better than you did a few days ago,' he said, raising his hand, palm open. 'High five?'

Ross slapped hands with him, grinning from ear to ear. 'I wanted to say thank you for getting me out of the mine,' he said. 'I was really scared, and I didn't think anyone would come to get me.'

James nodded. 'I can imagine how you must have felt down there. It was pitch black and you were in a lot of pain. But luckily for you, your brother sounded the alarm...so we came and found you as soon as we heard.' James looked him over. 'How are you feeling?'

'I'm okay.' Ross made a small frown. 'They give me tablets for the pain, and someone comes to help me exercise my legs. I can walk a bit on crutches, but the nurse says it might take a few weeks before I'm back on my feet properly.'

'Yes, it can take a while, but you're out of bed and on the mend, and that's very good. I'm really pleased to see you up and about. Well done.'

'Yeah. I can't wait to get back home and see my mates.'

Sarah watched the interchange from the other side of the desk, where she was looking through her patients' notes on the computer. For all James had implied he didn't understand children too well, he seemed to be learning fast. He was naturally compassionate and it came across in his dealings with them.

It was plain to see that the child was still troubled by his experience, and clearly he was still in some pain, but, as James had pointed out, he was on the mend, and that was great news to hear. Ross's mother was smiling, happy to see her child lively and animated once more. They left A and E a few minutes later, with James promising to go and visit Ross on his ward.

'It's wonderful to see things turn out so well,' she said, and he nodded.

'That's the thing with children…they pick up so quickly. Perhaps it's because they're eager to get on with their lives, and they have so many things going on to distract them from their troubles.'

He came around the desk to look at the computer screen. 'This is Nicola Carter's file…so you're still keeping track of her?'

Sarah nodded. 'Some patients come into the emergency unit, get treated and then they're on their way, but with others it's not quite so simple. I want to know what happens to them after they leave us...like Ross, for instance. Technically, he's no longer our concern, but neither of us can resist checking to see how he's doing, can we?'

He laughed. 'True. So what's happening with Nicola? She was waiting for an appointment with the endocrinologist, last I heard.'

'She's already seen him and he arranged for her to have surgery to remove the tumour. He told her it was stopping the pituitary gland from functioning properly and that was why she collapsed and needed to be given steroid treatment. She'll be going to Theatre later today.' She frowned. 'I hope she'll be all right. She has a husband and three children, and they're all very worried about her.'

'I'm not surprised. Any surgery can be worrying, but for most people brain surgery's a frightening thing to contemplate. Let's hope the neurosurgeon manages to leave the pituitary gland intact. That way, it can start to produce the right amount of hormones and she at least has a chance of getting her life back.'

'From what I heard, he's new to the team...a youngish man, not very communicative.'

'Surgeons can be like that.' He gave a wry smile. 'They don't need to have much of a bedside manner when their patients are unconscious on a slab in Theatre, do they?'

Sarah had opened her mouth to answer him when Gemma came hurrying towards her. 'There's a problem with the patient you admitted to the observation ward—Ann-Marie Yates. Her boyfriend has just been in to see her and she's very upset, and now she's unwell again.' She shook her head. 'It's such a shame. Things started off all right. She's been fine since she was admitted, and we disconnected all the monitoring equipment as soon as we knew she was to be discharged this morning. She was getting ready to go home with her friend—apparently they share a flat—and then he walked in and they started to argue. And soon after he left, she collapsed again.'

'Oh, dear. She's not having too great a time, is she? Get her back onto all the monitoring equipment straight away and I'll come along and see her.'

'Okay. Thanks.' Gemma swivelled around, her sleek, black hair swishing as she hurried away.

James frowned, and Sarah jumped in before he had a chance to speak. 'I know you want me to refer her to her GP, but I still think we should investigate each episode thoroughly just in case there's something else going on.'

'I agree with you.' He said it in a calm, even tone, and she looked at him in surprise.

'You do?'

'You're an excellent doctor, Sarah. You've proved to me over these last few weeks that you're extremely competent, and the least I can do is go with your instincts. I'll come along with you to see how she is.'

She hadn't expected anything like that, but she was extraordinarily pleased and a little glow started up inside her. 'Okay. Thanks.' She led the way to the observation ward and arrived at Ann-Marie's bedside in time to see her struggling for breath and lying back against her pillows in a state of exhaustion.

'Hello, Ann-Marie,' Sarah greeted her. 'I can see you're unwell again. What seems to be the problem?'

'My chest hurts,' the girl whispered on a breathless note. 'I can't...breathe... I...'

'That's all right. Try not to worry. We'll give you something to help you feel more comfortable,' Sarah said in a reassuring tone.

'I'm...dizzy... I...' Ann-Marie's voice trailed off, her words becoming a jumble of incoherent sound.

'Let's get her some oxygen,' James said to Gemma, who had just finished taking the girl's blood pressure.

Gemma nodded and quickly went to fit a face mask over Ann-Marie's nose and mouth. 'Relax, and try to take deep breaths,' she told her.

'Her blood pressure's very low, and her heart rate is forty beats a minute and dropping,' Sarah said in a quiet voice. 'This isn't a straightforward emotional upset.'

'I think you're right.' James was studying the readout from the ECG machine. 'Her heart rate is way too low. We'd better put in an intravenous line and get ready to give her atropine. That should stimulate more output.'

Sarah was already seeing to that, but a short time later it was clear that the atropine wasn't working. Ann-Marie's heart rate had dropped even further and was at a dangerous level. 'We need the defibrillator on hand,' she told Gemma. 'I'm going to give her an epinephrine infusion, but if that doesn't work, we'll have no choice but to try transcutaneous pacing.'

It was a worrying situation. The electrical impulses in Ann-Marie's heart weren't stimulating the heart muscles to contract and pump blood around her body, and if her heart rate dropped any further she could soon go into cardiac arrest.

Sarah set up the infusion and they waited to see

what would happen, but after some time James shook his head. 'There's no change and we can't waste time trying any other medication while she's in this state. There's only one thing for it…we'll have to go ahead with the transcutaneous pacing after all.' He started to prepare sedative and painkilling medication while Sarah did her best to explain to their patient what they were about to do.

She couldn't be sure Ann-Marie was fully aware of what was going on around her, but she persisted in her efforts, saying, 'You might find this procedure a bit unpleasant, but we'll give you medication to help you feel more comfortable.'

James was already applying pads to the girl's chest and back, and Sarah started to set the controls on the machine. 'Okay, here we go. I'm starting the electrical impulses, low to begin with and increasing in strength until we have the rhythm we're looking for.'

'What's happening to her?' A man's voice cut into the tense silence of the room a minute or so later. 'Ann-Marie…'

Sarah glanced at him. He was in his early twenties, she guessed, tall, with unruly dark hair and anguished grey eyes.

'You'll have to stand back, sir,' Gemma said firmly. 'She's very poorly, and we need to get her condition stabilised before you can talk to her.'

'M-Marcus…?' Ann-Marie's voice was weak, but it was clear that she was coming round from her dazed state. Her blood oxygen level was improving as her heart began to beat a little faster, and a short time later

Sarah stopped the machine from emitting any more shocks.

'We have a normal rhythm,' she announced, relieved that the procedure had worked.

'Ann-Marie, I'm sorry,' the young man said. 'I'm here. I couldn't stay away. I was stupid... I thought... I thought you were seeing someone else.'

Gemma intervened once more. 'She needs to rest,' she told him. 'If you want to stay with her, you have to be quiet.'

He nodded, gulping back what he had been about to say. He hesitated. 'I'll just hold her hand...is that okay?' He looked around the room and Sarah nodded.

'If there's any sign that her treatment is being undermined, you'll be asked to leave,' she said. 'Am I making myself clear?'

Marcus nodded. 'As crystal. I won't do anything to upset her, I promise.'

Ann-Marie pulled the oxygen mask to one side and looked anxiously at James. 'Will I need to have that done again?' she asked in a breathless voice. 'What's happening to me?'

'It's possible,' he told her, 'but now we know what's happening we'll try to give you medication to regulate your heartbeat and avoid the necessity for such drastic treatment. From the looks of things, your heart's electrical system isn't working properly, so you might need to have a pacemaker fitted at some point in the near future.'

'Oh. I see.' She was struggling to take this in, but she glanced up at Marcus for reassurance. He gently squeezed her hand.

'In the meantime,' James said with a smile, 'we'll make arrangements for you to see a specialist. You don't need to worry about it. You'll be well looked after.'

'Thank you.'

Ann-Marie closed her eyes briefly, and Marcus pulled up a seat alongside the bed, continuing to hold her hand. 'How could you believe I'd go off with anyone else?' she muttered under her breath.

'I think we can leave her in Gemma's care for now,' Sarah said, her mouth curving as she sent James a quick glance. She finished writing up the medication chart and handed it to the nurse. 'Thanks for your help, Gemma.'

She walked back to A and E with James. 'Aren't you glad I didn't send her home yesterday?' she said with a crooked smile.

His mouth quirked. 'Rub it in, why don't you?' Then he sobered and said thoughtfully, 'I dare say I'd have come to the same conclusion as you if I'd examined her and taken a history. It goes to show you should trust your team.'

'Am I one of your team?' she asked softly. 'I'm still on probation, aren't I?'

'I think we both know what the outcome of that will be, don't we?' He smiled. 'Your job's safe, so you can relax as far as your future here is concerned.'

'I'm glad.' She gave a soft, shuddery sigh. 'It's a relief to know that you have faith in me.'

His gaze burned into her. 'I do, Sarah.'

Her green eyes glimmered as she returned his gaze. 'I'm just thankful one of my biggest worries has been taken away. I want to be able to tell the children their future is secure.'

James nodded and keyed in the security code to unlock the door to the emergency department. 'I've been thinking about that...especially about young Sam's worries. A lot's happened to him and Rosie in these last few months and maybe they both need a little more reassurance. It might help if we all spent some time together this weekend. What do you think? We could go down to the beach—try to get Rosie and Sam used to going down there once more. I know they have trouble with that...Rosie told me. Between us, though, we should be able to cope with any problems that come up.'

'You're making it hard for me to refuse when you put it like that,' she said.

'Do you want to refuse?' He sent her an oblique glance, looking at her keenly as though her response was all-important.

'No...not at all. An afternoon on the beach sounds like a great idea.' The idea of spending an afternoon with him was suddenly enormously attractive, and her heart made an excited leap inside her chest. She had to remind herself that he was only doing this for the children.

'Good. I'll come to your place around lunchtime on Saturday. It'll be good to spend time together. We could perhaps start off by having something to eat at the local inn?'

'I think that would be lovely.' Inside, she was bubbling with anticipation. 'I'll look forward to it.'

By the time Saturday came around, Rosie and Sam were eager to be off. Sam swivelled around in his seat by the computer. 'Will we be going in James's sports car?' he wanted to know. 'I wish I could drive it. It's well good.' He started to turn an imaginary steering-wheel with his hands and made brumming sounds like an engine roaring off into the distance.

'I expect so. The inn is a couple of miles from here, so I doubt we'll be walking.' She frowned, glancing around the room. Rosie was rummaging through a hold-all on the dining-room table, anxious to make sure that all the preparations were in hand, but Sam was being his usual self, oblivious to any need to do anything other than play his game.

'Are you two about ready?' she asked, fetching coats from the hall cloakroom. 'Come away from that computer, Sam. You need to find your beach shoes if you're going on the sand—I don't want you ruining your best trainers. Make sure you put them in your bag. And find your swimming stuff.'

'Aw...can't you do it for me?' Sam protested. 'I'm in the middle of this war game. We're holed up in a cave in the mountains and the rebels are coming after us.'

'No, I can't. James will be here in a few minutes and I still have to go and look in the shed for buckets and spades. You can put your swim trunks on under your clothes. Save the game and play it later, or I might have to switch you off at the wall socket.' She came over to the computer table and let her hand hover over the plug.

'Spoilsport,' Sam complained. 'I'm nearly up to level ten...another few minutes and I'll have cracked it.'

'Crack it some other time.' Sarah waited while he saved the game and then she switched off the computer. 'Rosie, put a couple of bottles of pop into the backpack for me, will you, please? We're bound to need a drink down on the beach.'

'Okay.' Rosie went to do as she asked, and Sarah followed her into the kitchen, on her way to the back door.

'Are you all right about this afternoon's trip?' she asked. 'We don't need to stay for too long if it bothers you, but I thought it would be nice for you to have the chance to splash in the sea for a bit and maybe play ball with Sam on the beach.'

'I think so. I don't know.' Rosie looked up at her, a variety of expressions flitting across her face. 'I feel a bit peculiar inside.' She slid bottles and tumblers into the bag and glanced at Sarah. 'It'll be different, though, going with James. I like him. He showed me how to set up my new dance game when he came to do the fireplace in my room, and when I was cross with Sam for being a nuisance, he took him away and helped him with his war game.'

'Yes, I've noticed he's good at finding solutions to things.' James didn't make a big song or dance about anything, but somehow or other he managed to smooth the path whenever there was a problem.

She went out to the shed and rummaged around for a bit. It was full of stuff from the children's former family home in Devon, as well as bits and pieces that Sarah had brought with her.

A few minutes later she went back to the kitchen with her hands full of buckets, spades, plastic sieves and a large beach ball. She was startled to see James standing by the table, talking to Rosie. As she entered the room his glance skimmed over her.

'You look great,' he said, his eyes lighting up, and her

cheeks flushed under his avid scrutiny. She was wearing jeans that clung where they touched and a simple, short-sleeved top that outlined her curves. He was equally casually dressed, in dark jeans and a T-shirt. 'Rosie let me in,' he said. 'She told me you were almost ready, but apparently we're waiting for Sam to find his shoes.'

'Except he's upstairs playing on his game pad,' Rosie commented drily. 'Shall I go and tell him to hurry up?'

'Better not, or there's bound to be a fight. You could find some tissues and put them in my handbag, if you like.' Sarah smiled. 'I'll go and see what Sam's up to in a minute when I've found a home for these buckets and spades.'

'I'll put them in the boot,' James murmured. He grinned, looking at the bags and accumulated paraphernalia. 'Are you sure you haven't forgotten anything… folding table, portable gas stove, water canisters?'

'Oh, very funny,' she retorted, flicking him a pert glance as they went out to his car. The top was down, reflecting the warmth of the summer's day. The sky was blue, with no clouds in sight, and the air was fresh and clean. 'Like I said before, you've no idea how much preparation goes into a trip where children are involved.'

'Obviously not. Though we are only going for the afternoon, you know.' There was a glint in his eye as he gave her a sidelong look. 'Unless, of course, you wanted to make a weekend of it. It's not beyond the realms of possibility that we could go for longer…there's a lovely Smugglers' Inn along the coast where they do rooms.'

There was a hint of devilishness in his voice, sparking her pulses into a throbbing beat. He wasn't being

serious, of course, but even so, she had to take a moment
or two to calm herself down before answering him.

She carefully arranged the buckets and spades to one
side of the car's boot. Then she looked at him, raising
finely shaped eyebrows. 'It isn't going to happen. I'm
not seventeen years old any more, you know. I hope
I've a little more sense than to go throwing myself at
you as I did back then.'

'No? Are you absolutely sure about that?' He was
teasing her now, with laughter in his eyes and a rogu-
ish smile playing around his mouth.

'Definitely not. That was a big mistake. I can't think
what came over me...and it certainly won't happen
again.' She went hot all over, thinking about how she'd
pressed her soft curves up against him and wound her
arms around his neck. Her green eyes narrowed on him.
'Besides, I seem to remember you saying something
recently about keeping things on a professional footing between us.'

'Hmm.' His mouth made a downward turn. 'I guess
I've been fooling myself about that all along. I must
have had a change of heart somewhere along the way.
Perhaps seeing you in total command of yourself in A
and E over these last few weeks has made me realise I
should never have insisted on the three-month trial period in the first place. I was being over-cautious.'

'I'm glad you think so.' She moved away from the
car as Rosie came out with the bags. 'Sweetheart, you
should have left those for me,' she said in consterna-
tion, seeing her struggle with the weight.

James took the bags from Rosie and loaded them
into the car. 'You did well to manage these,' he said. 'I

was just telling Sarah she's packed everything bar the kitchen sink.'

Rosie chuckled. 'She wants to make sure everything is just right. I think she would have packed a hamper, but you said we were going out for lunch, didn't you?'

'I certainly did.' He glanced at the expensive watch on his wrist. 'And I think we should be getting on our way. Is there any chance of dragging your brother out of game paradise, do you think?'

Rosie shook her head. 'I don't think so. He doesn't even listen after he's loaded it up.'

'Uh-huh...we'll see about that.' Sarah went to fetch him, and within a minute or two they were all installed inside the car and were on their way. The children were hungry and already debating what there might be to eat, and Sarah admitted that it had been a long time since breakfast for her, too.

'I had a slice of toast before the children were up, and ate it while I skimmed my emails and read through my letters. They were a bit disappointing really, just bills and a printed estimate for the roof repairs.'

'Were you looking for something more?' James drove along the coast road, and Sarah leaned back in her seat, enjoying the feel of the breeze riffling her hair. The children were absorbed in watching the gulls circle the bay and trying to count how many boats were moored in the harbour.

'I was hoping there might be something from my mother.' She winced. 'I checked the marriages for the postmarked area over the last few years, and there weren't all that many with my surname and my mother's first name. So I followed them up, and I think I've found her.'

James shot her a quick glance. 'That must have come as a bit of a shock after all this time. Did you find an address?'

She nodded. 'Yes. I wrote to her, and I've been waiting to hear ever since. I gave her my email address and my phone number.' She sighed. 'There's been nothing so far. I keep kidding myself that she might be on holiday, or that I have the wrong person, but I suppose I have to accept that the truth is she probably doesn't want to know.'

'I'm sorry.' He clasped her hand in his briefly, keeping one hand on the steering-wheel. 'I'm not convinced that getting to know her again is such a good idea, anyway. As time's gone by you've been gradually getting your life back together, and I can't help thinking that if she turns up you'll find yourself drawn into an emotional whirlpool all over again.'

'It was never going to be easy, was it? Anyway, from the looks of things, it probably won't come about.'

They drove on for a while, until they came to an attractive, seventeenth-century inn, set back from the road. James parked the car and Sarah took a moment to look around at the white-painted building. It had lots of sash windows and there were hanging baskets at the front, filled with red geraniums and bright petunias. Wooden tables and chairs were set out on the forecourt, each group with its own red umbrella, and there were stone tubs dotted about, laden with flamboyant, crimson begonias and trailing foliage.

'Have you been here before?' James asked, and she shook her head.

'No, I haven't, but if the outside is anything to go by, it's lovely.'

'I asked the landlord to reserve a table for us by a window,' he said, shepherding the children out of the car and along the path. 'We can eat and look out at the sea at the same time, and if Sam and Rosie are finished before us, they can go to the play area at the back of the pub. We'll be able to see them from where we're sitting.'

'That's great.' She sent him an approving glance. 'It sounds as though you've thought it all out.'

He nodded. 'I want you to have a good time and be able to relax for a while.'

'Thanks.'

They went inside, and Sarah admired the low, wooden beams and the huge fireplace filled with logs. There was wooden bench seating on two sides, made comfortable with luxurious padded upholstery, and tables and chairs were grouped in cosy, recessed areas brightened with the golden glow of wall lamps. There was some raised decking, and their table was on one of these sections, by a tall, wide window that allowed daylight to pour into the room and gave them a beautiful sea view.

'Seafood's the specialty here,' James explained, handing her a menu, 'but there are all sorts of other dishes for you to choose from.'

'I want the chicken nuggets,' Sam decided, with the speed of lightning.

'As if you ever eat anything else.' Rosie studied the

menu for a little longer. 'Could I have gammon and fries, please?' she asked.

'Of course, whatever you like.' James looked at Sarah, his dark brow lifting in query. 'What would you like?'

'I'll have the sea bass,' she said with a smile. 'They say it's cooked with lemon, ginger and honey. Yum... it sounds delicious.'

'It is. I can recommend it.'

James chose the same, and they spent a pleasant hour enjoying the good food and looking out over the coastline, watching the waves roll gently into the bay. They talked about all sorts of things—the times when Sarah had been learning how to climb rocks, and her job in Devon when she'd gone out and about with the ambulance service. James told her about his efforts to do up the house he'd inherited, and of his visits home, when he helped his brother with the running of the farm estate.

'The orchards are massive, aren't they?' Sarah commented. 'I remember when I worked there in the summer holidays there were tons of apples to be picked. And you would come round with scrumpy cider for all the workers when we were on our lunch breaks.'

'Mmm... Technically, you weren't supposed to have it. It was pretty lethal stuff. But I think I gave you just a taster and made up the difference with orange juice.'

She laughed. 'Yes, I remember that now. I was so cross at the time.'

'You were cross about a lot of things back then.'

'Why were you cross?' Rosie asked, and Sarah gave a small start. She had forgotten the children might be listening in.

'It was because my mother had gone away,' she said quietly. 'I thought she should have stayed.'

Rosie frowned. 'Why would that make you cross? Our mother went away, but we were sad about it, not cross.'

Sarah took a moment to think how she should answer that. 'Yes, of course, that's understandable. But your mother didn't have a choice. Mine did. She chose to go away. She didn't want to stay.'

Sam's gaze was troubled. He reached out and patted her hand. 'It's all right, Sarah. We're here for you now.'

Sarah's eyes misted over at his innocent, sweet gesture of compassion. She blinked hard and swallowed against the lump that had formed in her throat. 'That's good to know, Sam,' she said huskily. 'I'm glad I have you and Rosie.'

James sucked in a deep breath. 'What more could anyone ask?' He smiled at the children and then glanced at the debris of crockery that littered the table. 'Except maybe for lots of ice cream and strawberry sundaes...'

'Yay...I'll have one of those!' Sam exclaimed. 'Can I?'

James nodded. 'They do them with fresh strawberries.'

'Yummy, scrummy, scrumptious,' Rosie said happily. 'They're my favourites.'

'Mine, too.' James gave their order to the waitress, and then glanced at Sarah. 'Are you okay?' he asked in a low voice. He reached for her hand, and folded it within his own.

'I'm fine.' She nodded. Rosie and Sam were busy colouring in the pictures on the printed sheets of paper that the waitress had given them and weren't taking any notice of what she and James were doing. 'I'm glad they feel the three of us belong together. Little gestures like that make it all worthwhile somehow, don't they?'

'They do.'

The children finished their desserts and Sarah sent them out to play on the climbing apparatus for a while. She and James took a few more leisurely minutes to drink their coffee, and turned the conversation to good food and wine.

When Sam and Rosie tired of the small adventure playground outside, they gathered up the baggage from the boot and headed down a winding path towards the beach. Here there were smooth stretches of sand broken up by rocks and boulders scattered around the base of the cliffs, and the children headed over to the rock pools with whoops of delight.

'Did we bring the fishing nets?' Sam asked, and Sarah had to shake her head.

'Sorry, we didn't.'

'You can use the small buckets to scoop things up,' James said. 'Here, let me help.' James walked alongside Sam, looking in the pools left behind by the tide, searching for crabs and other small crustaceans, while Rosie stayed with Sarah, picking up shells and examining patches of seaweed that had been washed up by the sea.

Later, the children slipped off their outer clothes and ran into the sea in their swimming gear, splashing in the shallows as the waves broke on the shore, before venturing further out and jumping with the bigger waves that came along. 'That's far enough,' Sarah told them. 'Stay close by the shore.' She and James rolled up their jeans and went into the water with them, laughing as an unexpected wave drenched them from the knees down.

James slid an arm around her waist and helped her run back to the shore as another wave threatened to overtake them. Still laughing, they dropped on to the sand, looking out over the sea to where the children played.

James was still holding her, and Sarah was content to lean back against him, folded into the crook of his arm. It seemed so natural to be with him this way, and as the sun warmed her bare arms and dried out her jeans, she thought how good it would be if the afternoon could go on for ever.

It couldn't, of course. As time went by, a breeze blew up, and Rosie and Sam were getting cold and ready to scramble out of their wet things and into their dry clothes. Sarah covered them in beach towels and helped them to get dressed, and then they all trooped back to the car.

'That was terrific,' Rosie said, settling back in her seat and lifting her face to the gentle wind as James drove them home.

'Especially the rock pools and the ice creams,' Sam added. 'The crabs were well good. I saw ten. Wait till I tell Ricky. He'll want to come as well next time. Can we bring him with us one day?'

'I expect so.' Sarah lifted her brows as she turned in her seat to look at him. 'Does that mean you're best friends now?'

'Yeah.' Sam didn't volunteer any more than that. He drew his game pad out of his pocket and concentrated on the screen.

Sarah smiled. 'I guess I shouldn't have worried,' she murmured, and James chuckled.

'I guess not.'

They arrived home a few minutes later and the children disappeared into their bedrooms. Sarah flicked the switch on the coffee percolator and started to set out mugs for her and James.

'I had a great time this afternoon,' she said, smiling at him as he came to stand beside her.

'So did I.' He wrapped his arms around her, drawing her to him and lowering his head so that his forehead lightly touched hers. 'It was good to hold you, out there on the beach, but I wanted to do so much more than that.'

'You did?' She looked up at him, her green eyes questioning. She trailed her hand lightly up across his chest, her fingers coming to rest on his powerful biceps.

'Oh, yes,' he said, his voice becoming rough edged, his lips hovering close to hers. 'I've tried so hard to keep my distance from you...physically, at least...these last few weeks, to avoid touching you or getting too close to you, but I'm fighting a losing battle. I know how much you worry about getting involved, but whenever I'm near you I want to kiss you and hold you and show you just how much I want you.'

'I'm glad,' she whispered. 'I want you, too.'

His body reacted instantly, as though she'd delivered him an electric shock. His hands pressed her to him, tugging her even closer than before and she gloried in the feel of him, in the way their bodies fused, one into the other, her soft curves blending with his taut, muscular frame. Her fingertips slid upwards into the silky hair at the nape of his neck, and she clung to him, loving the way his arms encircled her. His thighs moved against hers and his hands began to make a slow detour over her body, worshipping each and every rounded contour.

A shuddery sigh escaped her as his hand tenderly cupped her breast, and he covered her mouth with his, cutting off the soft groan that formed in her throat.

Hunger surged in her, raging through her body like a firestorm, and as he lovingly caressed her she realised, through the haze that filled her head, that he must feel the same way. His heart was pounding, so much so that she could feel the thunderous beat of it against her breasts, and the knowledge filled her with a heady, tingling exhilaration. He wanted her every bit as much as she wanted him.

'I need you, Sarah,' he said huskily. 'I'm glad you're not seventeen any more. I don't know how I can go on without you...' His heated gaze swept over her, burning in its intensity, and he kissed her again, his hands roaming over the swell of her hips and easing her against him until pleasure built up in her and threatened to spill over in wave after wave of heady, tantalising desire.

'I want...' She started to say something, to tell him how much she wanted him, too, but something disrupted the heightened tension in the atmosphere, piercing it as though it was a pocket of hot gas that had built up and was ready to explode.

'What was that?' James suddenly became still, frowning as he, too, sought to find out where the disturbance was coming from.

They heard hissing, popping and bubbling sounds that were coming from behind them, and Sarah said in a bemused voice, 'It's the percolator.' She looked at James. 'I'd forgotten all about it.'

'Me, too.' He reluctantly eased himself away from her so that he could turn it off, and would have reached for her once again if it hadn't been for Rosie coming into the kitchen at that moment.

'Can I use the laptop?' she asked Sarah. 'I want to see if my friends from Devon are on line, but Sam's on the other computer.'

Sarah pulled in a deep breath, trying to get back to something like normality. She sent James a quick, sorrowful look. The mood had been broken, and they couldn't get back to where they'd been. He inclined his head briefly, sadly. Perhaps he felt it, too.

With the change in atmosphere, along came a niggling doubt. James hadn't wanted her all those years ago. Why did he want her now? Were his feelings purely a physical response?

'Yes, that's okay.'

Rosie sat down by the table and ran her fingers over the keyboard. There was a tinkling sound, and she said, 'Oh, you have some emails. They've just come in.' She glanced up at Sarah, her grey eyes wide. 'I think there's one you've been waiting for. The heading says, "Getting in touch".'

'Uh... I...' Sarah felt winded all at once, and a little dizzy. Her head was still up in the clouds somewhere from being with James, and now this had come at her, out of the blue.

She couldn't think what to do, and it was James who said quietly, 'I think you'd better sit down and read it, don't you? I'll see to the coffee.'

She floundered for a moment or two and then managed to find her voice. 'Okay, thanks.'

Rosie smiled. 'I'll come back in a couple of minutes, shall I? I'll go and text my friend from school while I'm waiting.'

'Yes, that's a good idea. I won't be long.' Sarah sat down and opened up the email. It was short, just a few lines, and she read through it quickly. Then she frowned and stared at the screen, not knowing what to think.

'What's wrong?' James asked, his expression guarded as he slid a mug of coffee towards her.

'I... Nothing, really. I mean, she's got back to me... my mother...which is what I wanted after all.'

'But? There is a but.'

'I'm not sure.' She read the email once more.

'Doesn't she want to meet up with you, is that the problem?'

'No. I mean, yes...she wants to see me. She's suggesting that I go over to London and have lunch with her some time at a local restaurant. She doesn't have a lot of time to spare, she says.' She looked up at him. 'That's okay, I suppose, isn't it?'

It wasn't quite what she'd expected. Maybe she'd been hoping for something with a little more warmth, an expression of joy at being able to link up with her after all this time. Not this cool, brief invitation to lunch as though she was a mere acquaintance who'd happened to drop her a line. She was her daughter, but she might as well have been a stranger. Sadness clouded her eyes. It was like being abandoned all over again. Was she really so undeserving of love?

James looked at her with concern, and he put his mug

of coffee down on to the worktop next to him. 'You're asking me if it's okay? I don't know, Sarah. My instincts tell me it isn't, and from the look on your face, you feel the same way. Is that all she says? After all this time it doesn't feel as though it's enough. Not by any means.'

Sarah pressed her lips together. 'Well, she wants us to get together, and that's what I wanted after all. Only...I think I'd expected something more.'

A muscle flicked in his jaw. 'Of course you did. She walked out on you, her only child. She's made no effort to find you through all these years, and now she can't even be bothered to go to the trouble of coming here to see you? I'm sorry to be blunt, but at the very least she might have suggested you stay over at her place for a couple of days.'

'Perhaps she's afraid we won't get on. Or maybe she has a family of her own now.'

'And you aren't her family? Who has the better claim?'

'Even so...'

Exasperated, he came over to her. 'May I read what she has to say?'

'Of course.' She nodded and turned the laptop around so that he could see the screen.

A second or two later he sucked in his breath. 'Sarah, please tell me you're not going to dignify that by agreeing to go and have lunch with her. That's the chilliest invitation I've read in a long time. There's not even an expression of regret for what she did. You deserve so much better than that.'

She ran the tip of her tongue lightly over her lips. 'It might not be such a bad idea to go and see her. At least it would be a start.' He made a stifled sound, and she added, 'I'm not sure what I'm going to do yet. I have to think about it.'

'What is there to think about?' His voice was terse, reflecting the anger in his expression. 'She has the nerve to say that she's busy and can't spare you much time. She has a business to run...an online business, for heaven's sake, selling handbags and fashion accessories. How difficult can that be? Doesn't she know you're a doctor, working weekends sometimes, out on call at other times too? Did you tell her that?'

'Yes, I did. I told her quite a bit about myself and about my father and the children. I was sort of hoping she'd tell me more about herself.'

'The woman is selfish, Sarah. Always has been, always will be. Perhaps you should face up to the fact that she isn't going to change. When are you going to realise that you can't let her ruin your life any longer?'

'Like I said, I have to think about this.'

He shook his head, as though he was trying to rid himself of the whole idea. 'I almost wish she had never answered your letter. This is going to stir everything up all over again, isn't it? You were doing so well, getting yourself back on track, and now she's going to drag you down into her cold, self-centred world once more. She'll destroy you, and make you feel worthless all over again. Hasn't she already started the process with that wretched little note? I can see how badly it has affected you.'

He moved restlessly. 'I'd hoped there might be a chance for us...for you and me to get together, for us to be a couple. But you'll never settle to that, will you?

Oh, it might be all right for a while, but there will always be doubt at the back of your mind, won't there? The worry that you'll be abandoned all over again?' He looked into her eyes, his gaze searing her. 'You know I want you, Sarah. Do you think we have any kind of a future together?'

Her lips parted as she tried to answer him. She'd waited so long to hear him say that they were a couple, that they would be together... Of course she knew he wanted her. He'd made that clear over the last few weeks, the way he'd been there for her, cared for her. But he was right, there was always a niggling doubt in the back of her mind that things would not work out for them. How could he love her, and want to be with her for ever? Had he ever mentioned love? And what of the other women, from the hospital and other walks of life, who'd set their hearts on him and had had their hopes and dreams dashed? Was she to become another one of them?

'James, you have to understand, it's hard for me to trust, to put my faith in anyone. I've been badly hurt, and I don't know how to put that behind me. I try, but something always gets in the way. I don't know how to change. You said once that being abandoned was like a scar on my mind, and maybe you were right— perhaps it has damaged me for ever.'

He sighed heavily. 'Then I guess I have my answer, don't I?' He turned away from her, picking up his car keys from the worktop. 'There's no hope for us.'

'James...'

'I'm sorry. I have to go. I can't do this any more. I have feelings too, you know.' He was already striding towards the door. 'I need to get some air and maybe drive around for a bit. You must do what you think right where your mother is concerned.'

He walked out, and Sarah sat at the table for a while after he had gone. What had been a wonderful day had turned to ashes, and for the moment she didn't have any idea how to deal with the aftermath. She stared into space, wishing with all her heart that James had stayed, that she'd been able to give him the answer he wanted.

'James has gone. You were arguing with him, weren't you? I heard you.' Rosie was shocked, and there was disbelief in her voice. 'How could you let him go like that?'

'We weren't arguing, Rosie. We were just…'

'You were. I heard you. Your voices were loud and he was angry.' Her face crumpled. 'Now it's all gone wrong.'

Sarah stood up, seeing the distress in Rosie's face. 'Rosie,' she said gently, putting an arm around the small girl, 'it wasn't an argument, not really. We just don't agree on some things, that's all. Sometimes grown-ups have differences of opinion. It's all right to do that.'

'No, it isn't,' Rosie sobbed. 'I like James. I wanted him to stay. We could have been a family, and now it's all ruined.'

Sarah hugged her, shocked by all those expectations that had been slowly simmering beneath the surface. She glanced across the room and saw Sam standing in the doorway. 'Did you feel that way, too?' she asked quietly, and he nodded, white faced.

'I wanted him to stay as well.'

'I'm sorry.' She held out an arm to him and he came

into her embrace. They were echoing her own thoughts, but right now there wasn't a thing she could do about it.

Her mother's leaving had always been at the heart of her problems, making her uncertain, insecure and feeling unloved…unlovable. James had been dealing with that for some time, and now he'd decided enough was enough. He'd gone, and things might never again be the same between them. She couldn't bear it.

CHAPTER EIGHT

SARAH'S pager went off, alerting her to an incoming emergency, and she winced inwardly. She was looking after a man who had suffered an angina attack and she really didn't want to leave him right now. He was frightened, fearful of the pain and desperately worried about what was happening to him.

'The nitroglycerin spray will help relieve the pain,' she told him. 'It widens the blood vessels and helps the heart pump blood around your body more easily. Just try to breathe slowly and evenly, and it should soon start to pass.'

She glanced at the nurse who was assisting her, and said in a quiet voice, 'I have to go and attend to another emergency. Will you stay with him and make sure that he's comfortable?' She reached for the medication chart and made some notes. 'I've written up his medication, but if there are any problems, call the registrar. He's due to take over from me in half an hour.'

The nurse nodded. 'I'll take care of him.' She held the oxygen mask to the man's face. 'Take it nice and slowly. Deep breaths. That's right. That's fine. You're doing really well.'

Sarah glanced at the ECG printout and saw that the

attack was receding. 'You're in good hands,' she told her patient. 'You should feel better very soon.'

She hurried away, heading for the resuscitation room, and found herself walking swiftly alongside James. Her heart seemed to clamp into a tight knot inside her. She'd hardly had a chance to speak to him all day, and it looked as though they were still going to be tied up with work now, when it was nearly the end of her shift. There was so much she needed to say to him but here at work their conversation was muted, constricted by their surroundings, by work and the constant bustle of colleagues all around them.

'It looks as though we've both been paged for the same case,' he said with a frown.

'Yes. Do you know what it's all about?'

He shook his head. 'I was dealing with an appendicitis case—it's been non-stop all day.'

'You're right. I didn't even get to stop for lunch.'

'It goes like that sometimes.'

'Yes.' She sent him a quick glance. 'I tried to phone you yesterday, but all I got was your messaging service telling me you'd been called out to the hospital. It looks as though the rush started yesterday for you.'

'I had to come in to do some emergency surgery.' He pushed open the door to the resuscitation room and Gemma hurried to update them on the situation.

'This is Lucy Myers. She gave birth to a baby girl about eight hours ago. She was sent home as normal, but she became unwell and started to bleed heavily so her husband turned the car around and brought her straight here to A and E.'

'And the husband is…where?' James glanced around as he went to introduce himself to the young woman.

'In the relatives' room with the baby.'

'Okay.'

Lucy was already connected up to the monitors via various pads and electrodes, and it was plain to see from the readings that she was in a bad way. She was being given oxygen through a face mask but appeared not to be aware of her surroundings.

'She complained of dizziness and feeling faint,' Gemma said, 'and she's suffering from palpitations. It's hard to estimate how much blood she's lost, but from her condition it's a fair amount, I'd say.'

James spoke quietly to their patient, trying to calm her down and let her know that she would be safe. It was difficult to know how much she was able to take in, because the loss of blood was having a system-wide effect on her. 'I'm going to take some blood from your arm so that we can see if there's anything to pinpoint what might be causing this,' he said. 'But you had a prolonged labour, from what the records tell me, and that can sometimes lead to problems like this.'

Sarah made a careful examination and gently palpated the woman's abdomen. 'It looks as though the uterus isn't contracting as it should,' she murmured. Usually, after the placenta came away, there would be some bleeding, which would gradually stop as the womb contracted and compressed the blood vessels.

James relayed that information to Lucy. 'I'm going to put in an intravenous line so that we can give you fluids to help make up for what you've lost, and at the same time give you medication to help make the uterus contract,' he said.

Lucy didn't say anything. She was conscious, but too exhausted and debilitated to take any notice of what was going on.

'She's not responding too well, is she?' Sarah remarked softly. 'I've been massaging the uterus, but it hasn't helped to stimulate the contractions.'

'No.' James checked the monitors. 'Her heart rate's far too high. I'll give her oxytocin and see if that starts things off.' He turned to Gemma. 'Alert Obstetrics and Gynaecology, will you, please, Gemma? They need to be aware of what's going on.'

'Will do. Do you want me to have Theatre on standby, too?'

He nodded. 'That would be for the best. I'm hoping it won't come to that, but it's possible she'll need surgery to stop the bleeding.' He frowned. 'You'd better talk to the husband about the possibility—he might have to sign the necessary consents if his wife isn't up to it.'

'Okay.'

James gave Lucy the medication through the intravenous catheter, and then he and Sarah stood back away from the bed for a while, waiting to see if her vital signs improved.

Sarah stretched, easing her aching muscles. It had been a long day.

James glanced at her. 'Are you okay?'

'I'm fine.' He seemed calm and relaxed, and there was no sign of any tension in his manner towards her. She wanted to talk to him about what had happened between them on Saturday afternoon, but this was hardly the place to do that. Instead, she kept to safe ground, talking about their work. 'I checked on Nicola Carter this morning,' she told him. 'Apparently the tumour was benign.'

James smiled. 'Yes, I read her notes. That must be a great relief for her family.'

'I imagine so.'

'What's happening with the girl you were worried about? Rachel, the one who had a bad reaction with Ecstasy?'

'She's doing much better. Her heart rhythm has settled down, and it's possible she'll be discharged soon.'

'To go back to her old lifestyle?'

Sarah shook her head. 'I don't think so. Her brother put her in touch with her parents, and from what I heard they all had a heart to heart and managed to sort things out. I think she'll be going back home to live with them.'

'That's good.' His gaze swept over her. 'At least somebody's family has been put back together again.'

'It goes to show that it's possible sometimes.' She lifted her chin. 'It all comes down to both parties making an effort to meet each other halfway.'

'Yeah, maybe.' He checked the monitors once more and went to carefully examine Lucy. 'The uterus is still soft and relaxed, and there are no contractions,' he said, under his breath. 'We'll try one more medication and if that doesn't start things off, there's nothing else for it—she'll have to go up to Theatre for surgery to clamp the blood vessels.'

'What are you going to use? Methylergonovine?'

'Yes. It might mean she won't be able to breastfeed for a few days, because it could pass into the milk, but

I don't see that we have a choice.' James was already preparing the intravenous injection.

Once the injection had been given, they waited once again for it to take effect. 'Perhaps her husband could come in now?' Sarah suggested in a low voice. 'If this works, it would be good for her to see him and the baby…it might help with the bonding process. She had a long, exhausting labour, and then she collapsed, so she's had very little time to hold her baby. The midwife said she wasn't able to hold her for more than a minute or two because she was so weak.'

James frowned. 'So why was she discharged after only a few hours?'

'They had no beds and a couple of emergencies came in. I don't think they had much of a choice, once her temperature and blood pressure were okay.'

His expression was sombre. 'The days are gone when new mothers would at least stay in hospital overnight.'

He went over to the bed and examined Lucy once more. 'The uterus is contracting,' he told Sarah. 'It looks as though her condition's about to stabilise.'

Lucy gave a low moan and stirred briefly. Then her eyelids flickered open.

'Hey,' he said softly, 'you're back with us. That's terrific. Are you okay, Lucy? How are you feeling?' The monitors showed that her blood oxygen level was up and her heart rate was gradually coming down to a more normal level.

Lucy nodded, pushing the oxygen mask to one side. 'I'm okay,' she said in a thin, tired voice. 'What happened to me? I feel wiped out.' Then, anxiously, 'Where's my baby?'

Sarah smiled. It was great that she was asking after her newborn infant. 'She's on her way. Your husband is looking after her. The nurse has gone to fetch them.'

The husband arrived in Resus a few minutes later, armed with a fresh, warm bottle of milk formula for the baby. 'I think she's hungry,' he said, looking down at the squalling infant in his arms. 'She's been asleep all this time, and then she suddenly woke up and all hell was let loose. She has a good pair of lungs on her and that's no mistake.' He smiled at his wife, and went to stand beside her. 'The nurse went to fetch the milk for me.'

Lucy held out her arms for the baby, and he carefully lowered the crying infant down to her. She snuggled her close in the crook of her arm and tested the milk for heat against the back of her hand. Then she gently eased the teat into the infant's mouth and there was instant peace in the room, with only soft sucking and gurgling sounds coming from the contented baby.

Sarah watched them, a tender smile on her lips. There was a hint of sadness in her expression too, though, and James looked at her curiously and murmured, 'It's good to see them together like that, isn't it? We'll let her recover for a while and then admit her to the observation ward.'

She nodded, but didn't say anything. They started to walk out of the room. Their job here was finished, and she could go home now, secure in the knowledge that their patient was out of the woods.

He asked quietly, 'Is something bothering you?'

'Not really. But I can't help wondering how my mother felt when she held me for the first time. Perhaps she never experienced that glow of motherhood. For her, having a baby might have been a burden, something that she felt she had to do to please her husband.'

His brows shot up. 'What makes you think that? Have you spoken to her about it?'

'We've exchanged a few emails. She says she never wanted children. She wanted to have a career, but my father was keen for them to start a family, so she went along with it.'

'Good grief.' His expression was bemused. 'I'm surprised she would admit to something like that.'

She gave a faint smile. 'I had pretty much the same thought, but I'd asked her to be honest with me, so I suppose I can't complain. Anyway, I'm going home now, so I'll be able to see if she has anything else to say.' She glanced at him as she reached for her purse from a locked cupboard behind the central desk. 'Will you be going off duty soon?'

'In about half an hour.' He caught hold of her arm as she would have walked away, gently circling it with his fingers. 'Sarah, I was wrong the other day when I suggested you shouldn't go and see her. It's not up to me to say what you should or shouldn't do. You have to do what you think is best. I just don't want to see you hurt.'

'I know. I understood that.'

'I'm glad.'

He might have said more, but Gemma called him to go and look at a patient, and Sarah made her way out of the department and set off for home. She was sad because her mother had turned out to be not quite what she'd expected, but at least she was in touch with her now, and gradually they would begin to get to know one another.

Now that she was over the initial shock of making contact, she'd realised that what bothered her most of all was not how she and her mother would go on but the state of her relationship with James. When he'd walked out on Saturday, she'd been lost, as though she'd been cast adrift.

She collected the children from Murray's house, and took them home to give them tea and biscuits to stave off the hunger pangs while she prepared the evening meal.

'Don't go eating too many, Sam,' she warned as he went to dip his hand in the biscuit barrel for the third time. 'I know it's been quite a while since lunchtime, but it's important that you eat all your dinner.'

'What are we having?'

'Beef risotto.'

'No problem. I love it.'

'Even so…' She replaced the lid on the biscuit tin as his fingers began to stray once more. 'You've had enough for now.'

'Can I fry the onions?' Rosie asked. 'I know how to do them until they're golden brown.'

'Okay.' Sarah smiled. Inside, she was aching a little for all that might have been, but Rosie and Sam kept her from thinking too hard about that. Whenever she was in danger of sinking into thoughts of James and how things could ever work out the way she wanted, one or other of them demanded her attention. 'Let's see, we need onions, mince, a little garlic…'

'Tomatoes and peas,' Rosie added.

'Yes, you're right.' She checked the items off one by

one as she placed them on the kitchen table. 'I think that's about everything, don't you?'

'It won't be any good without the rice,' Sam said, frowning. 'Whoever heard of risotto without the rice?'

Sarah laughed. 'It's a good job you're here to keep me on course, isn't it?'

He gave them both a smug smile, and then went off to his bedroom to play for a while.

Some twenty minutes later the appetising smell of risotto filled the kitchen. 'We'll give it another fifteen minutes or so,' Sarah said. 'That'll give you time to do some colouring or—' She broke off as the doorbell sounded. 'It can't be Murray,' she said with a frown. 'He said he was going out this evening to have dinner with his girlfriend.'

She went to the front door and found James waiting in the porch. 'Oh…hello,' she said, her heart giving a small leap inside her chest, a smile curving her mouth. 'I thought…well, it's good to see you.' She waved him into the hallway, but he stopped, standing still and sniffing the air approvingly.

'Something smells really good,' he said. He looked uncomfortable. 'I didn't mean to barge in on you when you were about to sit down to your meal.'

'That's okay. You can stay and eat with us. We made plenty.'

He followed her as she walked towards the kitchen, and Sarah glanced up as she saw Sam flit across the landing upstairs. 'Hi, James,' he said, and then disappeared into his room once more.

Rosie greeted him with a sweet smile. 'Hi,' she said.

She stared at him for a while and then added, 'I was afraid you might not come here again.'

'Oh, why's that?' James frowned.

Rosie's shoulders did a strange little wiggle. 'Because you and Sarah had an argument last time.'

'No...no...' He glanced at Sarah, his expression sombre. 'That was just a bit of a difference of opinion, that's all.'

'That's what Sarah said.' Smiling happily, she went to join her brother upstairs.

Sarah listened for a moment or two, waiting for them to start arguing, but nothing happened, and she turned to James. 'I'm really glad you came,' she said. 'I was miserable when you went away. I wanted to see you again, to talk to you properly, without worrying about being at work with people all around.'

He came over to her and took her in his arms. 'I was thinking exactly the same thing. I thought I should stay away, but I can't. I need to be here with you.'

'You're not still cross about my mother getting in touch?'

His mouth flattened. 'That was the least of my worries. But I think I was afraid that you would always be living in your mother's shadow, worrying about why she didn't care enough to stay, and it seemed such a waste. All these years you've been scared that there was no future for you, that you wouldn't have a family of your own because in the back of your mind you felt you didn't deserve it. You have to know that you can enjoy these things the same as everyone else. Your mother didn't reject you—she rejected the idea of motherhood. It doesn't mean that you're unlovable.'

'I think I'm beginning to realise that.' She pressed her lips together briefly. 'I don't know what I was hoping for...to find some reason that turned her against me and my father, I suppose. But it wasn't that after all. It was simply that she never wanted a family. She wanted a career and freedom to do as she pleased without being tied down. And one day it all became too much for her, so she left to go and live her life the way she'd always wanted to.'

He ran his hand lightly down her arm. 'I'm sorry. Have you decided what you're going to do? Will you go and see her?'

'Maybe, one day, but not for some time. I thought it would be better to take things slowly. We can exchange emails, photos, get to know one another that way, and then perhaps we can talk on the phone at some point. I'm still not sure quite how I feel, but somehow it's as though a weight's been lifted off me. I really thought there was something wrong with me, and that she'd walked away from me...but now I know that she's the one with the problem. It's made me look at things in a whole new light. It made me think that I was wrong in believing none of my relationships could ever work out.' She looked up at him. 'I mean, I was wrong in thinking things would never work between you and me.'

He exhaled slowly. 'I'm glad you've come to realise that. I was hoping you would see things that way, but I didn't think it was possible.' His arms circled her, wrapping her in his warm embrace. 'I care about you so much, Sarah. I want you to know how I feel about you, but I needed you to know that things can be good between us. Everything doesn't have to turn sour.'

She lifted her face to him, her eyes troubled. 'I know you want me, but I don't really understand what you feel for me. You didn't want me when I was a teenager... you turned me away then...so what's changed? Why is now any different? I'm still the same person—a little curvier perhaps, not so impulsive and reckless, but basically I'm still me.'

'Ah, Sarah...' He bent his head and dropped a kiss on her startled mouth. 'I always wanted you. It took every ounce of willpower I had to turn you away that night. But I had to do it. You were so young and vulnerable, so confused... After your mother left, you put on this tough exterior, but I knew it wasn't for real, you were a young girl crying out for attention, and I couldn't take advantage of you. I wanted you more than anything, but I knew you'd hate me the next day, perhaps for always.'

He frowned. 'Besides, I had to go away to work. It wasn't as though I could stay close by. You had your future ahead of you. I knew you had to get rid of the demons that were driving you before you could settle to any kind of relationship.' He gave a rueful smile. 'I just didn't think it would take this long.'

She stared at him in bewilderment. 'You're saying that you wanted me back then? That you've wanted me all along?'

'More than that. I love you, Sarah. I couldn't let you know. I didn't want you to fling yourself into a relationship with me then realise you'd made a mistake and blame me later. I wanted you to be sure of your feelings. I love you and I'll always be here for you. That's why I've never been able to settle into a relationship with anyone else. You're the only woman I've ever loved.

I'll never leave you, you need to know that, but do you think you can conquer your doubts?'

Joy welled up inside her. She lifted her arms, wrapping them around him, and lifted her face for his kiss. 'I've always loved you,' she said. 'I never had any doubts about that. I was afraid you wouldn't be able to love me in return.' She made a choking little laugh. 'I was such a pain back then. I think I wanted to do my worst to prove to myself that no one could possibly love me.'

'It didn't work,' he said. 'It just made me want to protect you all the more.' He kissed her tenderly, brushing his lips over hers, trailing kisses over her cheek and along the smooth column of her throat. 'I love you and I want to spend the rest of my life with you.'

Her eyes widened. 'Do you really mean it?'

'I do.' He gently stroked her cheek, gazing down at her. 'Will you marry me, Sarah?'

She smiled up at him. 'Yes, please. It's what I want more than anything.' But then her expression sobered as she thought of something else that might be a stumbling block to mar their happiness. 'You realise, don't you, that it means you'll be taking on not only me but Rosie and Sam as well?'

'Oh, I think I can cope with that,' he said confidently, swooping to kiss her once more. 'We'll be a family, you, me, Rosie and Sam. You won't need to worry about anything.'

She snuggled against him, wrapped securely, satisfyingly in his arms, and for the next few minutes they were lost in one another, oblivious to everything around them. Sarah sighed happily. It was exhilarating, being held this way, having him kiss her and show her just how much he loved her. She wanted this moment to go on for ever and ever.

EPILOGUE

'ARE you ready? Do you have everything you need? Something old, something new...?' Sarah's mother fussed around her, adjusting the folds of Sarah's ivory silk wedding gown and carefully draping the lace edged veil over her bare shoulders. 'Oh, you look so beautiful. I just can't believe... I never imagined I would see this day.' She wiped away a tear with the edge of her white handkerchief.

'Something old...' Sarah fingered the silver necklace she was wearing. Her father had given it to her when she had been a bridesmaid at his wedding, and she had treasured it ever since. 'Something new...' She smiled. 'James bought me these earrings to wear.' She turned her head this way and that, to show them off.

'They're lovely, absolutely exquisite.' Her mother's eyes were misting over once more.

They were diamond droplets, with an emerald at their core. 'To match your beautiful eyes,' James had said, and Sarah's mouth curved at the memory. 'Something borrowed, something blue...that's how the saying goes, isn't it?' She glanced down at the white silk ribbon that tied her bouquet of pink roses and fragrant orchids. 'I'll give this back to you later. I understand how much it means to you.' She hadn't understood the significance at first, but when her mother had explained that it was the ribbon from Sarah's christening gown, tears had come to her eyes. After all that had happened, her mother hadn't been able to part with this one tender memento of her baby girl.

Her mother nodded. 'I'll have new memories to treasure after this, though, won't I?' A line creased her brow. 'Can you ever forgive me, Sarah? Getting to know you all over again, and seeing you with James and Rosie and Sam has made me realise how badly I've behaved and just how much I've been missing. I'm so proud of you.'

'I forgive you,' Sarah said softly. On this day, of all days, she was thinking only of the future...of the wonderful, love-filled life that she was going to share with James.

Her mother sighed heavily, the breath catching in her throat. 'Thank you. It's more than I dared expect.' She frowned as a car drew up outside and there was a knock at the door. 'Oh, the taxi's here... I have to go.' Her voice rose in agitation. 'Where are Sam and Rosie? They have to come with me.'

'It's all right, we're here, we're ready,' Rosie said, coming into the sitting room. 'Murray was showing us pictures of the seaside where he's taking us for the next two weeks—him and his girlfriend. I like her, she's fun...and there are caves and rock pools and lots and lots of sand.'

'It'll be well good,' Sam joined in. 'He says we can go on sail boats and try out body surfing and stuff.'

'I think you'll have a great time,' Sarah said. 'But you'd better phone me every day, or else,' she warned.

Rosie laughed. 'We will.' She gave a twirl, showing off her pink silk dress and letting the skirts billow out around her. 'Do I look all right?'

'You look stunning, as pretty as a picture.' Sarah turned to Sam. 'And you make a wonderful pageboy, Sam. You're so smart in your suit, and I love that silk waistcoat. Do you think you can keep it clean until after the ceremony?'

He gave her a nonchalant smile. 'Of course.'

Sarah saw them out to the waiting taxi and waved them off. In just a few short minutes she would be setting off herself in the wedding car, with Murray by her side to do the traditional 'giving away' of the bride.

She was suddenly overcome by nerves. Would James like the way she looked? What was he thinking right now? This was the biggest commitment either of them would ever make, and she wanted everything to be over with so that she could be with him, just the two of them for a short while, to start their new life together.

Some twenty minutes later she stood in the stone archway by the church door, calmly waiting while Murray, looking splendid in a morning suit, chivvied the children into their places behind her. Everything would be all right. She remembered the love token that James had given her to pin to the inside of her dress. It was a small silver hoop that held a trio of tiny charms— a carriage to represent their journey together through life, a silver horseshoe for luck, and the something blue—a sapphire heart, to show the love that he would always have for her.

The wedding march sounded out, cutting into her reverie, and she took Murray's arm, walking slowly down the aisle towards the man she was to marry.

James turned to look at her as she approached. His lips parted in stunned surprise, his eyes widening as he gazed at her, and then he smiled. At the same time the sun shone through the stained-glass windows of the church, lighting up the altar and the gleaming silver candlesticks and spreading its warm rays over the flowers that decorated the pedestals.

He came to stand beside her. 'You look sensational,' he whispered, clasping her hand in his, his grasp firm and assured. 'I love you.'

The vicar stepped forward. 'Dearly Beloved,' he said, 'we are gathered here today...' And the service began. Sarah glanced at James from time to time, and each time he responded, looking into her eyes, showing her all the love that was in his heart.

'With this ring, I thee wed.' James slid the gold ring onto the third finger of her left hand, and Sarah felt a lump rise in her throat. This ring bound them together for all time. It was what James had promised when he'd slipped the diamond engagement ring on her finger just a few short weeks ago, and now this simple act in the wedding service completed that promise.

He held her hand as he walked with her down the aisle a few minutes later, and they stepped out into the sunshine, to be greeted by cheering friends and family, who showered them with confetti and clamoured for him to kiss the bride.

He took her in his arms and obliged cheerfully, kissing her with a thoroughness that took her breath away

and pleased the onlookers enormously. 'My lovely wife,'
he said, some time later. 'I feel as though I've waited for
this moment for an eternity. I can't believe how lucky
I am.' His gaze travelled over her. 'From this day forward,' he murmured, quoting from the wedding service,
'I'll always be here for you, Sarah. Don't ever doubt it.'

'I won't,' she said softly. 'We'll be together, for ever.'

And then he kissed her again, to the great delight of
the photographer and everyone around.

* * * * *

A sneaky peek at next month...

Medical Romance™

CAPTIVATING MEDICAL DRAMA—WITH HEART

My wish list for next month's titles...

In stores from 5th October 2012:

❏ A Socialite's Christmas Wish – Lucy Clark

& Redeeming Dr Riccardi – Leah Martyn

❏ The Family Who Made Him Whole – Jennifer Taylor

& The Doctor Meets Her Match – Annie Claydon

❏ The Doctor's Lost-and-Found Heart – Dianne Drake

& The Man Who Wouldn't Marry – Tina Beckett

Available at WHSmith, Tesco, Asda, Eason, Amazon and Apple

Just can't wait?

Visit us Online

You can buy our books online a month before they hit the shops! **www.millsandboon.co.uk**

0912/03

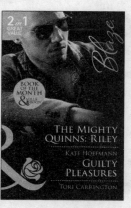

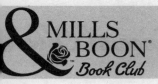

& *Special Offers*

Every month we put together collections and longer reads written by your favourite authors.

Here are some of next month's highlights— and don't miss our fabulous discount online!

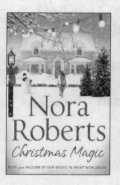

On sale 5th October

On sale 5th October

On sale 5th October

Save 20%
on all *Special Releases*

Find out more at
www.millsandboon.co.uk/specialreleases

Visit us
Online

1012/ST/MB3